Wolf Harbor

Wolf Harbor

To George my Dear, Dear Friend

Hope you Enjoy

Best Wishes

Alan Del Monte

Alan

05/24/10

Library of Congress Control Number:		2010903235
ISBN:	Hardcover	978-1-4500-5769-1
	Softcover	978-1-4500-5768-4
	Ebook	978-1-4500-5770-7

This book was printed in the United States of America.

To order additional copies of this book, contact:
Xlibris Corporation
1-888-795-4274
www.Xlibris.com
Orders@Xlibris.com
77660

CHAPTER 1

Martha Frost was a mess. Her life was unraveling, a fact she was painfully aware of. She was beyond angry. It didn't matter that at the tender age of twenty-eight, Marty, that's what her friends called her, was the toast of New York publishing. Six short years out of Cornell and she already had written three best selling murder mystery novels. It was the end of June 1943 and America was at war. Many fans had told Martha that her books were a source of pleasure and comfort to them in such troubled times. Yet here she was, "a sniveling whiney frump," the label she had given herself. "How is it an assistant professor of English Literature and Theater Arts at Columbia University and a best selling author to boot could sink to such depths?" she demanded. Her third serious relationship had just gone the way of the last two, crashing down in flames. "One for each best seller," she mocked. She could just imagine the headlines. "Successful Novelist a Bust at the Real Thing." Martha was not in the best of moods.

"Take some time, go up to Essex, Connecticut and stay with my Aunt Clara," was the advice her editor, Ellen Gold of Harcourt Press had suggested. "She's a great gal, and Essex is a wonderful place to get away from New York and recharge your batteries. You'll see, the time away will give you a completely new perspective. You will be itching to get back in no time."

"Oh yeah," thought Martha. "I'm sure that I'll be dying to get back to the origin of my doom. Essex is probably so damn boring," she told herself, "that even Manhattan will start to look good again."

Martha had no way of knowing she was about to be the star of her own murder mystery and she would not be the one to script the ending of this tale.

Ellen had booked Martha on the ten o'clock train to Boston out of Grand Central terminal in Manhattan. The first class lounge was comfortable and,

mercifully, there were only a few passengers. The kindly porter had tried to
cheer her up but Martha was not in the mood. Now she felt deep remorse
for being short with him. It was not her custom to be rude to service people.
The experience only served to make her feel bad, but no worse than she felt
every time she got a glimpse of her tear-swollen face in the window. The
image of the face looking back at her, now that was worse.

It had taken one hour and twenty minutes to reach New Haven,
Connecticut. Now it was only a short while before reaching Old Saybrook,
Martha's destination.

"Aunt Clara will have someone meet you at the station," said Ellen.
"This will be good for you, honey, you'll see."

"Easy for her," thought Martha. "She's not the one being banished
to the country." Martha was trying her best to put a positive spin on the
situation when she felt the train beginning to slow down. She almost had
herself convinced when suddenly seized with a fearful thought. "Oh no,"
she quietly exclaimed, "Who's going to do my hair?" ·

Martha slowly made her way to the rear of the car. The porter was waiting
with her luggage. He instructed her to wait while he lowered the metal steps,
securing them so she could make a safe descent to the station platform.

Martha made small talk with the porter, attempting to repair some of
the damage done earlier. The porter was very gracious and extremely grateful
for the twenty-dollar bill Martha pressed into his hand. This was wartime
and twenty dollars was a huge amount of money to a porter.

Now Martha was standing alone on the platform as the train pulled
away. She was beginning to feel stranded. She kept scanning the station in
the hope of making contact with her ride.

Just then, she heard the sound of screeching brakes and a car sliding to a
halt on the gravel surface of the station parking lot. A thin male made great
difficulty of getting out of the auto and headed in her direction. Martha
stared in disbelief as the driver who obviously had one bad leg half skipped
and half ran down the platform. With one arm flailing wildly while the other
tried to keep his hat from flying off his head, the Native American handyman
of Clara Tyler made his hilarious entrance into Martha Frost's life.

Martha just stood there. She looked up at the man's hat, best described
as a top view of Saturn with one of its rings.

"Nice hat," she deadpanned.

"I beg your pardon?" said the man, obviously taken aback by her
candor.

Once again, Martha stood silently. She was trying to decide whether to go with this person or go over to the other platform and simply return home.

"I'm James Whitefeather," offered the man, slowly catching his breath. "But people round here just call me Injun Jim. Come, let me take your bags so we can get to Clara's. She's real anxious to meet you."

With that, Injun Jim gathered up the luggage and started down the platform towards the car. Martha followed, still not believing what she was seeing. Martha was a city girl and she had to admit that meeting people like this Injun Jim, to say nothing of spending time in a place like Wolf Harbor, were foreign to her. Many of Martha's friends had accused her of being a snob. Martha took that as a term of endearment.

No sooner had Martha and her belongings been placed in the Chevy coupe, she found herself holding on for dear life as Injun Jim slammed the gear shift down and accelerated with great force.

"Big doings today," Jim shouted over the roar of the parking lot gravel spraying in all directions. The coupe charged out of the station and headed up route 9 to Essex and Wolf Harbor.

"Found a body by the old shipyard," he continued. "Some university fellow from Boston, Harvard I believe. Looks like he was murdered. Nothing like that ever happens in Wolf Harbor. Looks like you got here just in time."

"I'm here to rest, not get involved with local murders," Martha protested.

"Yeah, but I bet a smart lady like you could help the local cops a whole lot. These boys ain't much good at anything tougher than directing traffic," said Injun Jim with a laugh.

"Maybe you didn't hear me," Martha insisted, "I'm here to rest and only rest."

Injun Jim got the message. Already, he was not feeling too kindly towards Aunt Clara's guest. He decided to keep his thoughts to himself as he headed down Main Street towards Aunt Clara's residence.

Martha admired the stately homes lining the main thoroughfare, most of which were once the residences of the town's founders, all of them beautifully preserved, bearing markers to identify their early owners and the year of their construction.

"What a great setting for a novel," she mused but then brought herself back to reality. "I'm here to rest."

Injun Jim pulled the Chevy coupe into a driveway off Peck Street. A large three story white frame house sat peacefully surrounded by a perfectly manicured lawn. A flower garden in full bloom bordered the large wraparound front porch. Azaleas, chrysanthemums, and various perennials beautifully blended to complete the picture, a perfect representation of early Americana. The lawn and garden were the handiwork of this strange Indian fellow, Injun Jim.

A tiny young girl with a head full of barrel curl tresses flung the front door open, charged down the stairs and came to a halt on the lawn about ten feet from where the car came to rest. The little girl stood motionless without turning her gaze from the beautiful lady visitor who had come from New York City.

Martha was dressed in a simple skirt that rested just above her knees with a short-sleeved cotton blouse, both unassuming but obviously expensive. Considering the enormous impact the war had on the fashion industry, clothes of such quality were rare indeed. And, most certainly, they were not available in the far reaches of Yankee America where folks dressed sensibly. Lillith Tyler was star struck. The tall auburn haired lady with the fashionably coiffed hair looked like a movie star to the youngest of the Tyler children.

A tall elderly woman wearing a simple cotton housedress covered by a cotton apron came out of the house and approached Martha with two other children in tow. Aunt Clara introduced herself and welcomed her visitor to her home.

"I'll bet Injun Jim told you all about the excitement."

Martha acknowledged he had.

"That man is a regular town crier, I swear," declared Aunt Clara. "He's got more gossip in him than a group of women in a sewing circle."

Martha instantly took a liking to Aunt Clara. It was obvious who ruled the roost around here. Martha loved forceful women. She made sure that they were centerpieces in all her literary works.

"This young lady is my great-niece Mary," said Aunt Clara as she placed her arm around the ten-year old girl, the eldest of the Tyler children. Mary was tall for her age with a head of soft wavy blonde hair that fell past her shoulders. "And this is her brother Thomas," she said, pointing to the eight-year old middle child of Samuel Tyler. "And this little lady who can't seem to take her eyes off you is Lillith."

Struck by the scene before her, Martha, ever the writer, couldn't prevent herself from crafting a scenario. The house, Aunt Clara, three beautiful children, Injun Jim, it was all too perfect. Once again, she had to remind herself "I'm here to rest," only this time her thoughts were audible.

"Beg your pardon?" queried Aunt Clara, confused by Martha's words.

"Oh, forgive me," said Martha, "it's just a conversation I've been having with myself."

Aunt Clara gave her a questioning look. "Well if you're through talking to yourself, young lady," she said directly, "we can go into the house and get you settled in." With that, she turned and took the children in tow and headed up the front stairs. Injun Jim, taking hold of the luggage, gave Martha a weak smile and followed along.

Reluctantly, Martha slowly began making her ascent to join the others, but not without another silent discussion with herself. "Gee Martha; you're making one hell of an impression here, aren't you?"

The house was much larger inside than it appeared. A generous sized foyer gave way to a large parlor whose six-foot high windows allowed for streams of light to pour in. The centerpiece of the room was a large fireplace with a wide wooden mantel upon which there were many framed pictures of the Tyler family. Martha felt as if she had stepped back into the nineteenth century. The expensive, but well-worn furniture, dated back to the era when Essex was the home of well to do Yankee merchants and sea captains. Federal velvet upholstered pieces and Victorian horsehair sofas and chairs with antimacassars made for an eclectic, yet elegant mix. A couch and matching love seat framed the fireplace and Aunt Clara's hand-carved hickory rocking chair faced them both. The coffee table in the center of this grouping, as well as the mahogany accent tables covered in lace doilies and linens made by generations of Tyler women, were laden with beautifully framed family photos. The warmth of this lovely home was overwhelming. It was unpretentious but reeked of old money.

Aunt Clara gave Martha a tour of the house before showing her to her quarters on the third floor. Mary and Thomas ran out to the backyard to play, but Lillith was having none of that. Her attention was fixed solely on the mystery lady whom she found fascinating. Usually Martha found it uncomfortable being around children, but she found Lillith's attention curiously flattering.

The first floor had a huge eat-in kitchen, a dining room that comfortably sat ten for dinner, a pantry, sewing room, and a half-bath in the hall. The second floor had three good-sized bedrooms, which shared a full bathroom, also in the hall. Aunt Clara's suite had a large bedroom, a changing room with walk in closets, and its own private bathroom with irreplaceable antique appointments.

Martha was greatly surprised by the third floor quarters; a large bedroom bordered on one side by a pleasant sitting room and on the other by a changing room and bathroom exactly like Aunt Clara's room.

"My parents loved to entertain their friends who traveled some distances to visit them. They wanted their stay to be most enjoyable," said Aunt Clara. "As you can see there are many windows. My parents wanted their guests to enjoy the lovely view of Wolf Harbor as well as our Main Street. I hope you find your time here with us relaxing. I assure you, it is private up here. You will notice just to the left of the headboard is an intercom device. You can call down to the kitchen or to my quarters if you need to. We will call you only when necessary or at your request. Now, would you like to rest or join me for some of my afternoon tea? I take it on the back porch overlooking the harbor. It's really quite lovely."

"Tea would be wonderful if Lillith will join us," said Martha.

A look of extreme excitement came over Lillith's face. Hardly containing her joy, she shot a (can I, Aunt Clara please?) look in the older woman's direction.

"Well of course Lillith will join us," said Aunt Clara. "Come; let's go down to the kitchen."

Aunt Clara led the way down the back stairs to the kitchen. Martha's gesture toward Lillith was not lost on her. She had to admit, she was somewhat suspect concerning this city woman who was coming to visit, but now she wasn't so sure. By the time the women reached the kitchen, Aunt Clara had decided to wait just a little longer before passing final judgment. It'll be interesting to see if this woman was genuinely nice or smart and calculating.

The view of the harbor from the back porch with its magnificent yachting vessels was as lovely as promised. The only distraction was the large group of people gathered near the boathouse. There seemed to be vehicles everywhere. Most looked official. Just then, a tall man made his way to an unmarked black four door Ford sedan and removed his suit jacket. He loosened his tie and placed the jacket on the front seat of the vehicle. Next, he took hold of a handset and began conversing with someone on the other end. Finishing the conversation, he returned the handset to its holder, rolled up his shirtsleeves and began to head back to the boathouse. He stopped abruptly, turned, and took a few steps across the road towards the open land that was Aunt Clara's property. He looked up the hill and waved. Aunt Clara stood up, took a few steps down from the porch, and waved back.

"That's my nephew, Samuel Tyler, my brother Nathan's son. He's the children's father and Captain of the State Police Barracks down the road in Westbrook." Aunt Clara informed her guest. "He'll probably stop by to say hello before he heads back to the barracks. I'm sure the children have a million questions for him."

Aunt Clara's disclosure came as a surprise to Martha. Her friend Ellen had made no mention of a cousin who was a state police captain with three children. Things were beginning to get interesting.

"Sam and the kids live next door," said Aunt Clara as she pointed to the home just north of hers. Martha noticed the house was visibly larger than Aunt Clara's was. Aunt Clara anticipated Martha's next question. But, before she continued she asked Lillith to go to the kitchen to fetch Injun Jim, and some iced tea and glasses. Lillith joyfully obliged.

"Sam was married to Sally Templeton who died giving birth to Lillith. The Templetons are one of the wealthiest families in the area. They gave Sally and Sam their home as a wedding present. Their new home is up on the hill. It is much more suited to entertaining their elite acquaintances that literally come from all over the world to see them. Arlen Templeton is one of the few men not ruined during the depression. His money helped fund the ivory business down the road in Ivoryton and he is a key partner in Pratt Reed. The war economy has been good to the Templetons. They love Sam like their own. Sam and Sally had been sweethearts since the sixth grade. Of course, the Templetons have no reserve when it comes to Sally's children who just happen to be their only grandchildren. Those kids will never have a financial worry. Their trust funds are quite large and very secure. Arlen is a financial wizard. He and Betty moan a lot about Sam's refusal to allow them to spoil the children rotten, but deep down, I know they really admire him for it. The Templetons are good people. Arlen and his dad started out without a dime. They followed the great migration to California during the gold rush, but had the good sense to put their energies into the supply business. They made a deal with the Pacific Central Railroad people who bankrolled them. Both sides made a fortune. The Templeton's secret is simple. They find the needs of others and then come up with a way to supply those needs. Now it's the war. Heaven knows Arlen sure has done it again.

"Good Lord," Aunt Clara exclaimed. "Here I am standing here sounding just like that Injun Jim."

Speaking of Injun Jim, he and Lillith made their way onto the porch bearing a large pitcher of iced tea and glasses. Martha looked to catch Aunt Clara's attention as Lillith and Injun Jim placed them down, then Jim began to gather up the china to take to the kitchen.

"It's ok," Martha silently mouthed with a wink and a smile. Aunt Clara smiled back. A friendship between the two women was brewing.

"What a mess," came the words of Ethan Taft, Chief of Police of the Old Saybrook Police Department, the sole local police presence for Essex and surrounding towns. Taft's words were half disbelief and half nausea. The body lying at his feet bore the results of a skull battered by many blows.

"I guess whoever did this wanted to make sure the job was done," continued Taft.

"Either that or he was really in a pretty foul mood," offered Sam Tyler.

Chief Taft looked wearily at Sam who usually laced his comments with a generous helping of sarcasm, an inherited trait of the Tylers.

"Let's get him to the coroner in New Haven," said Sam. "Those doctors at New Haven Hospital will probably turn this into a standing room only seminar. I don't think those students have seen anything like this before."

"Yeah, and hopefully they won't see it again," said the chief.

"There's a damn war going on, Ethan, and some of those guys are going to end up over there. Think of this as Broken Bodies 101. It's just a prelude for them," reasoned Sam.

The chief shrugged knowing that Sam was right.

Sam left the crime scene, pulled his car into Aunt Clara's driveway, and parked behind the Chevy. He got out and walked around to the back yard. Mary and Thomas were the first to greet him. Thomas was the first to speak.

"Jimmy Collins said there was blood all over the place, Dad. Is it true?"

"Oh, Thomas," scolded older sister Mary, "must everything with you always be so ghoulish?"

"Well, that's what Jimmy said," Thomas protested.

"And it's real nice to see you too," said Sam, stepping in between his two oldest.

"Oh, Dad," Mary continued. "Thomas refuses to be civil. I swear he's demented."

"Swearing in front of our guest is not very nice," kidded Sam as he gathered his suddenly embarrassed daughter to his chest.

By now, Aunt Clara and Martha were standing looking down at Sam and the kids.

Lillith tugged at Martha's dress.

"They're always doing that," she informed Martha, with a look of exasperation. "Mary always tries to act like she's our mother and Thomas is so contrary."

"How old are you?" Martha asked.

"I'm almost five years old, but I'm much smarter than most kids my age," Lillith informed her.

"Oh, I'm sure you are," said Martha.

"It's almost scary, isn't it?" came the warm tones of Sam Tyler's voice.

Martha hadn't realized it, but Sam had made his way up onto the porch and now she and Sam were only a few feet apart.

"I'm Sam Tyler," he said while extending his right hand. "I assume you've met my children?"

At first, Martha said nothing, her silence creating nervous tension.

"Martha Frost," she blurted out finally. "And yes, I've met everyone, I think."

Before Sam could ask what she meant, Martha continued.

"I must admit, Ellen kept a lot of information from me. She probably figured the less I knew the better. I have to tell you that she made Essex seem quite dull, but restful, which is why I came. There seems to be a lot more here than I bargained for and Lillith is a pure joy."

"Come sit, Sam, and have some iced tea," beckoned Aunt Clara.

They sat and sipped their drinks while Sam filled everyone in on the death of the male in the boatyard below.

"I've read your books," Sam informed a surprised Martha. "They're very good. You have a keen sense of human nature. I really appreciate the touches of irony woven into your stories."

Martha was flattered.

"Of course I do wish you were a little more charitable to your police characters," Sam said with a laugh.

Now Martha became embarrassed.

"Oh, I'm sorry. It was only an observation, but I must tell you, I honestly enjoyed them all," Sam assured her.

Aunt Clara had been observing the two and noticed how Martha seemed to hang on to every one of Sam's words. Was it simply writers' interest or was it a woman's, she wondered?

Sam informed the group that he had to get back to the State Police barracks to file a report. He wouldn't be back for supper but Aunt Clara promised to send a plate home with the kids.

Sam got up to leave and extended his hand to Martha.

The warmth and gentleness of Sam's large hand pleased Martha. Sam headed to his car, leaving Martha to her own thoughts. She excused herself, climbed the stairs to her quarters to rest, and clean up for dinner. What a day it had been! Just about every preconceived notion she had about her visit had been wiped out in one short afternoon. She was sure this was going to be one interesting summer, not at all lonely and boring as she had imagined. Boy was she going to tell her old friend Ellen Gold a thing or two. The whole thing made her giggle with delight. "The Tylers of Wolf Harbor," she said to herself as she sat down on the side of her bed. Then there was Captain Samuel Tyler. For him she had only one word, "wow!"

CHAPTER 2

Martha awoke from a long restful sleep greeted by a room flooded with glorious morning light. The clock on the night table read nine-thirty. Martha nearly jumped out of bed; she never got up any later than six o'clock in the city. Suddenly, she caught herself as if struck by the realization of where she was; she stretched her arms up and out, and then allowed her body to collapse back onto the mattress. Her mind slowly drifted back to the past evening and dinner with Aunt Clara and the children.

On her first evening in Wolf Harbor Martha participated in a long, time-honored Tyler tradition of dinner with Aunt Clara. Of course, there were times when Sam had to work, but most evenings were a family affair at Aunt Clara's house. School was out for the summer, so the children stayed until eight o'clock. Then it was home and to their rooms. Mary and Thomas were allowed to stay up until ten o'clock, but Lillith had to be asleep no later than nine o'clock. Ella Mae Rucker, the Tyler's housekeeper, had been with them ever since Sally Tyler had died. Ella Mae was invaluable. She came every day at eleven a.m. to put the house in order and to prepare lunch for the children. Her day usually ended at five p.m., but on nights when Sam had to work late, she stayed until he got home. Ella Mae's husband, Marvin, drove her there and picked her up. Like Aunt Clara, she never saw the need to learn how to drive an automobile. Ella Mae had four grown children who lived in the area. There was always someone around to give her a ride if necessary. Her fifth and oldest son, Henry, was a lieutenant in the Army Air Corps seeing action somewhere in Europe. Her youngest, Robert, was another story. The Ruckers had done an admirable job of raising their four oldest, but somehow it all went sour with Robert. Marvin Rucker blamed himself for overindulging their youngest, as he was a full eight years younger than his nearest sibling was. Robert was a truant and a regular thorn in his parents' side. His many scrapes with the law, while all for petty crimes, were beginning to make him a household name at Old Saybrook police headquarters. News of him started to reach the state police barracks. Sam did what he could to help, but he had to agree with many of the locals that this young man was hell-bent on destruction.

Martha got an earful of gossip from Aunt Clara who, of course, never gossiped. Aunt Clara magically covered a monumental amount of territory in just a few short hours. Martha fell in love with her. She also found all three Tyler children to be delightful. It didn't take much inquiry to discover why Mary and Thomas were at the top of their respective classes at school. Mary was all about literature and she quoted Louisa May Alcott verbatim. Thomas's interests were in science. Nothing made sense to Thomas unless it made sense; you had to prove everything. The elder Tylers were hoping this was just a phase, one that would mercifully pass sometime soon. Then there was Lillith. As far as Martha was concerned, Lillith was the most beautiful child on earth. When Lillith spoke, her whole body spoke. Her eyes, her mouth, and every part of her little body went into motion.

Later that evening as Martha soaked herself in the claw foot bathtub, she closed her eyes and played the last eight hours over in her head. What a day it had been! Never in her life had Martha felt so immediately accepted, so welcome. The idea just made her feel good all over. She smiled and sank deeper into the water.

Martha finally collected herself, splashed water on her face, put on some makeup, slacks and a blouse and made her way down to the kitchen.

"Well, young lady, it sure looks like you got some needed rest," said Aunt Clara cheerfully as she was working on her third cup of morning coffee. "Are you ready for some breakfast?" asked Aunt Clara.

Martha couldn't believe the words, "I could eat a horse," came out of her mouth. Breakfast was usually no big deal to her back home. "Maybe it's the air?" she reasoned to herself. Aunt Clara had already sprung into action. Bacon, eggs, toast with fresh local jam and coffee were foreign concepts to Martha. Nevertheless, she devoured them. Martha ate and Aunt Clara talked. Martha sensed that this was going to be a recurring theme and then she thought, "Dear Lord, if I eat like this over the next six weeks, I'll be able to float back to New York."

Just then, Sam walked into the kitchen. Aunt Clara was surprised.

"This is a pleasant surprise," she said.

"I'm on my way down to the shipyard so I thought I'd pop in and say hello."

Martha was suddenly feeling stuffed. "Is my face swollen?" she began to panic. She began to look for a hole in the wide plank kitchen floor to crawl through. "How could he do this to me?" she demanded. "Get hold of yourself, Martha," she told herself.

"How are you feeling today?" asked Sam. "Did you get a good night's sleep?"

Words came hard to Martha. Her actions seemed to be two paces behind her mind. Finally, Martha managed a weak smile. "It was very restful," she managed, hardly audible.

"You can bet it was, Sam," said Aunt Clara. "A few minutes ago she was wolfing down her breakfast like pigs in a silo."

Martha wanted to die. Miraculously she composed herself and began to speak in intelligible sentences. Sam seemed relieved. He really had a problem with tightly wound people. They took themselves too seriously, he thought. Maybe there was hope for this lady yet. She sure was attractive. It suddenly struck Sam that this was the first time since Sally's passing he had felt this way.

"Got to get down to the boatyard," he informed them finally. "By the way, I saw the kids up at Zuckerman's," he informed Aunt Clara.

"They went to meet some friends. We're going to have a picnic over at Lacey's Pond this afternoon. I'm sure Wanda won't mind. She's so busy with that darn restaurant she hardly sees those children anyway. Now don't forget tomorrow night," Aunt Clara reminded Sam. "Injun Jim looks forward to this for a whole year. The kids do, too."

"No problem," said Sam. "I'll be home around six which will give me plenty of time to change and help you out."

Sam left for the boatyard and Aunt Clara filled Martha in.

"Its July 4th weekend and we celebrate in a big way. The town holds a large celebration on the town green with rides for the kids and all kinds of activities. There's a big fireworks display and lots and lots of food. You'll get a chance to meet the whole town. It's really something. Of course, you probably see more excitement every day back home, but for us here, this takes the cake."

"I'm sure I'll love it," said Martha. "By the way, what's going to happen tomorrow night?" she asked.

"Oh, tomorrow night belongs to Injun Jim. We Tylers hold a campfire cookout for the local children. It's another one of our Tyler traditions. Indian tales told by Injun Jim are the highlight of the evening. That man knows his stuff and he has a real flair for the dramatic. The kids love it, but so do the adults. You'll meet the mayor and his family and some of the local bigwigs. Don't worry; I'm sure you'll charm them. Just be prepared, though, they'll probably ask you a million questions about being a successful writer and life in New York City. The excitement might be too much for some of them. Just relax. You'll see, they'll be more nervous than you," Aunt Clara assured her.

Martha escorted Aunt Clara up Main Street to Zuckerman's to check on the children. The air was so fresh, and everything was quiet and tranquil. As they walked, Martha couldn't shake the feeling of not missing New York. If anyone had told her a week ago this was going to occur Martha would have had a good laugh. This confirmed city gal was being intoxicated by the loveliness that was Essex, and now here it was eleven o'clock in the morning and Martha was sipping on one of Nathan Zuckerman's famous ice cream sodas. Right then Martha made up her mind she was going to walk everywhere, just as she had done in London, England, two years ago. The British literati wined and dined her, as she had never before experienced. Martha reasoned that she consumed more food and spirits in one week in London then she usually did in a month. The common denominator had been all the walking she had done. By the third night there, her legs were aching. She toughed out the week and to her surprise found she had lost three pounds in the process. From that day on Martha adopted a much more pedestrian lifestyle. If she could get there by walking then that's what she did. Even her friend Ellen Gold told her walking had transformed her figure. Living in a congested city like New York definitely had its pluses and Martha took full advantage of them.

Sam met up with Chief Taft at the boatyard to check on any progress. "I got a list of the people staying at the Griswold," he informed Sam. "Six patrons checked out in the last twenty-four hours. It's going to take some time before we can reach them all. You'll have to use your contacts in New York, Michigan and Louisiana to run background checks on these people. The innkeeper at the Gris said she saw nothing unusual or odd in their behavior. We'll have to cross-reference to see if there is any way any of them had dealings with the deceased, Professor Weiss. You might want to reach out to anyone you know in Washington. No one seems to know why the professor was here. He was supposedly on his way to New Haven, probably Yale. There's been a lot of talk going around about some sordid doings down there. I wouldn't be surprised. It's not the first time the government hooked up with those college folks, using a conference as means of getting people together. But there was one thing about Professor Weiss that sounded a little funny."

Sam was all ears. "Yeah, and what was that?" he asked.

"It seems the professor was carrying a lot of cash and was pretty open about it. I found out that he ate up at the Black Swan the other night so I went to see Wanda. She confirmed the story and told me that the professor was loud spoken for a college guy. She said it seemed like he was going out of his way to draw attention to himself."

Sam took it all in, but was most concerned that it was more than twenty-four hours into the case and things were yet to connect or add up. The war had taken many good men from the ranks of the police across the country and information was harder to come by. It would take a few days, maybe a week just to track down Professor Weiss's fellow guests at the Griswold. Sam had some friends at the New Haven Police Department from the summer baseball games organized by the various police departments in the local towns. A real rivalry had developed over the years between competing towns from New Haven to New London. This would be the first summer with no games; there just weren't enough players. But Sam had made many friends and those friends had friends. It takes some time to set up a network, but Sam knew he had to be patient. He was sure there was no danger to the locals. Patience and persistence would be his greatest allies.

Sam had a nagging feeling that this case had "international affair" written all over it. It was just an intuition. He really had nothing to go on, but something right off the bat told him this was no local crime. The Harvard-Yale connection seemed plausible when you added all the war manufacturing done in the area, some of which was secretive.

That night Sam and Martha took the children up to the area to observe the traveling carnival people bringing all their equipment in by trucks and trailers. As they walked, Sam filled Martha in concerning the submarines being built in Groton, just north of them, and of the secret gliders being manufactured over in Deep River.

"I find the whole concept of those gliders just fascinating," Martha said to a startled Sam.

"Just what do you know about them?" Sam inquired.

"Well, let's see," Martha began. "I know they have an eighty-foot wing span and that Pratt Reed and Company is using a new type of construction called modular or prefabricating in the design. I know an aeroplane pulled up by a three hundred foot pulley rope that propels the plane is carrying it up. Once airborne it can fly some distance until it has landed behind enemy lines. Each ship carries eight soldiers, one of whom also doubles as its pilot. It's quite a remarkable idea and is useful to the war effort when carrying out covert operations."

"Just how?" Sam started to ask.

"Thomas," was Martha's reply.

"Thomas," responded Sam. "I'm going to have a word with that boy."

Martha pleaded with Sam not to scold Thomas right now with all the activity going on. "Please don't be upset," she said. "I'm afraid he was trying to impress me this afternoon. He really is remarkable, Sam. Remember, I'm a writer, not a reporter. I swear I won't breathe a word of this to anyone."

Sam thought for a moment then continued walking. Mary, Thomas, and Lillith had met up with some of the other children and their parents who had come to watch the carnival people arrive. Sam was quiet which made Martha slightly nervous. In the midst of Martha's disclosure, Sam could not get over that walking with this beautiful visitor was one of the more enjoyable things he had done in a long time. Thomas's indiscretion had mildly upset Sam but all he wanted to do now was enjoy Martha's presence.

"This woman is going to go back to her life at some point," Sam told himself. "And I'm sure that I, and my children, will just be a pleasant memory of an enjoyable summer interlude in her busy and exciting life." That's what he told himself and he really believed it until he felt Martha place her arm around his and draw closer as they walked.

Sam got home at six o'clock as promised and was soon helping the family prepare for the evening's festivities. Injun Jim had really outdone himself. He had set up a wigwam and decorative totem poles. He prepared a large campfire for later in the evening when all the invited guests gathered around to listen to his storytelling. Spread all over Aunt Clara's lawn were two large barbeque pits, tables and tents for food and the guests.

Martha couldn't believe how much she enjoyed helping out. She, Aunt Clara, Injun Jim, and the children were in constant motion the whole day. The caterers had come to set up the tents and storage facilities and a few neighbors came over to offer assistance with the stringing of the lights.

The family, including Martha, greeted their guests who started arriving at around seven-thirty. It wasn't long before Mayor Tinsley arrived with his wife, Abigail, and thirty-year old unmarried daughter Allison. Martha noticed the firm, almost viselike grip of Allison's hello handshake. Allison was smiling, but Martha knew the meaning behind that painted smile. All of a sudden, Martha was sensing she was operating on someone else's turf. It was a little while later that Mary informed her that Allison Tinsley had staked out her dad ever since her mom had died. No one came between Allison and the object of her affection, Sam Tyler.

"I'd watch my back when she's around," Mary informed her. "Allison is used to getting what she wants. Her daddy does everything he can to make his little girl happy. My guess is the Tinsleys are going to be nice to you in public, but they might view you as an enemy. Enemies of the Tinsleys usually don't fare well around these parts."

Martha just stared at Mary with a look of disbelief. She wasn't sure what to respond to first. Here she was, a major journalist from the big city, but she honestly didn't know what to be more frightened of, the powerful Tinsleys or these outrageous Tyler children.

"You're really ten years old?" she asked Mary with a tone of disbelief. "Never mind," she said before Mary could answer. She just shook her head and then took Mary's hand to go join the others.

"What do you feed your children?" Martha inquired of Sam.

"I don't think I understand your question," answered Sam.

"They're wise beyond their years," said Martha.

Sam began to laugh. "They're wise beyond my years," he said.

That got a laugh out of Martha, too.

"I know, I know," he said. "I have no idea where they come up with half of the things they come up with or half the things they do, but you have to admit, they're not boring."

Martha fully agreed, "Scary, not boring, but definitely scary."

Just then, a large shriek came from the direction of the campfire. A huge fire had risen up at the Indian campsite. Aunt Clara made her way over to where Sam and Martha were standing.

"Good Lord," exclaimed Aunt Clara. "What's that fool Injun Jim done now?"

Just then, Injun Jim came scurrying away from the fire on his hand and knees. The concussion of the initial blast had knocked him off his feet. He hurriedly made his way over to Sam.

"Guess I kinda overdid it with my lighter fluid," he huffed. "Just trying to make an impression on Miss Frost, and all these important folks. I wanted this year's fire to be special."

Sam tried to keep his composure, but the sight of Injun Jim all frazzled was just too much fun to resist. "Well," started Sam. "It looks to me like you've met your objective."

"Huh?" questioned Injun Jim. "Oh, well yeah, I guess," was all he could muster.

Aunt Clara was not at all happy to see the huge fire that was burning almost out of control on her prized lawn. "You get that darn thing under control, mister, or I'm going to skin you alive," declared Aunt Clara.

Injun Jim looked pleadingly into Sam's eyes.

"Could you excuse me for a moment?" Sam said to Martha. "Jim and I have a slight problem to attend to."

"Go ahead," Martha responded. "Aunt Clara and I will gather up the children and meet you there."

It took a few minutes, but the fire gradually reached a safe level and the large crowd of guests eagerly formed a circle around Injun Jim's campsite. The town's children always looked forward to Injun Jim's campfire tales, as did the adults. Martha soon realized that Injun Jim was good at these things.

A hush came over the crowd as Injun Jim began.

"Well, folks, many, many years ago, before we became a nation there was another nation that was already here. Actually, there were many nations here known as the Sioux, Iroquois, Apache, Narragansetts, the Paugussetts, the Pequots and the Mohegans, to name a few. In these here parts, the two largest tribes were the Mohegans and the Pequots. Back in the early sixteen hundreds, not long after the Mayflower colony came to be, a war broke out between the settlers and the Pequots known as the great Pequot War, and it lasted three long years. The two main characters of our story are Sassacus, the chief of the Pequots and my great ancestor, Uncas, the chief of the Mohegans. Now the Mohegans were a pretty crafty bunch. Uncas could see that the settlers were not going to go away and that a great number of them were sure to be coming over here to this new land. The Mohegans quickly became friendly with these new people. Old Chief Uncas was one smart fellow. He knew the British military was close by and the Mohegans could never survive a conflict that included fighting the British. The Pequots, on the other hand, were a warrior tribe, greatly feared by Indians and settlers alike. What's more, the Pequots were a real unfriendly bunch. Those people refused to be hospitable to the settlers and pretty much kept to themselves. Things started getting a little scary when old John Winthrop, the governor at the time, signed a treaty that would force the Pequots from their land along the river. The Dutch were the first to engage the Pequots, who refused to move. They managed to capture the Pequots' Chief Tatobem and hold him for ransom. The Pequots paid the ransom, but the Dutch killed Tatobem anyway. This sure did not make the Pequots happy, to say the least. And what's more, the Pequots weren't about to go without a fight. Killing their chief just about destroyed any possibility of trust between them and the Dutch. Well, it didn't take long for the Pequots to take their revenge. Under new Chief Sassacus, they attacked the Dutch trading post, the Hope near Hartford. Then they got their allies, the Western Niantic, to kill John Stone, a Virginia trader. Sassacus was a pretty shrewd cuss. He promised to turn over Stone's killers to the English and to open up safe trade routes. The English sent John Oldham, an English trader, thinking everything was all right, but it wasn't. The Pequots killed Oldham too, and now it was the Brits who were not happy.

These killings by the Pequots led to the English calling them a blaspheming, murderous, lying bunch of heathens. They went so far as to call them Satanic and declared a Holy War against them saying the outcome could only be satisfied by the total annihilation of those evildoers.

The English started to attack them in earnest. Meanwhile Sassacus was having his problems keeping the Pequots united and his inability to enlist Chief Uncus and the Mohegans was causing further unrest within the tribes.

As I said, the war dragged on until finally, John Mason joined up with John Underhill and a group of volunteers and laid siege to the Pequot stronghold up at Mystic. During a sneak attack, they lit the whole place on fire but the defiant Pequots refused to come out. Uncas and the Mohegans had joined with the settlers and helped in the attack. Uncas knew one way or the other, the Pequots would lose and he was not going to see his tribe wiped out in an alliance with his unfriendly neighbor. Well, those Pequots were certainly brave or just plain stubborn; you'd have to be the judge of that. About six hundred men, women and children were burned to death in that fire."

A moan rose from the crowd as Injun Jim's words sunk in.

"And what's more, a good fourteen hundred Pequots died during that war. Survivors of the siege were killed or captured in the surrounding woods. Many were made slaves of the Mohegans and the other allied tribes while many were sent as slaves to the West Indies. In sixteen thirty-eight, the war finally came to an end with the signing of the Treaty of Hartford. The purpose of that treaty was to wipe the Pequots forever from the face of the earth. Well, folks; let me tell you that just didn't happen. To this day, the Pequots, what's left of them, are still here and danged if they still don't keep to themselves. A small group survived that war and swore they'd never trust anyone but their own kind again. Indians or whites, it don't much matter, they've spent over three hundred years isolating themselves from everyone. They still believe that someday they're going to rise again. And I'll tell you what, I'm not so sure they won't. Well, anyway, that's the story of the great Pequot War and how Essex came to be."

The crowd began to applaud, but Jim held up his hands to silence them.

"Because the Tylers have a famous guest in Miss Martha Frost and the mayor has brought some of his important friends up from the capitol along with his fine family, I'd like to tell you the story of how Wolf Harbor got its name. Would you like to hear that?" Jim asked the crowd.

The crowd responded as one. Everyone wanted to hear Injun Jim's account of the birth of Wolf Harbor. Injun Jim was only too happy to oblige.

"Well now," Injun Jim began. "In the mid-seventeen hundreds, before the war for independence, the Mc Clarron family moved into the area, and a nastier, more lawless bunch of hooligans never existed. The colonials had run the Mc Clarrons out of Barnstable, Massachusetts. Old man James Mc Clarron and his three roughneck sons, along with their wives and children, somehow ended up over on Methodist Hill, overlooking the point. Everyone soon learned that they were up to no good and when they tried to acquire a parcel of land on the river, the Lay family who owned most of it flat out refused them. What really galled the Mc Clarrons though was the fact that the Lay family had allowed a group of Christian folk who were new to the area to set up temporary living quarters in one of their large buildings on the wharf. The elder Mc Clarron was no fool and he knew that the land would be valuable for shipping and trade. Massachusetts already had many seaports and much shipbuilding so it stood to reason that trade was a natural for any town with a harbor and deep water. Potapaug, or Essex, as we know it today, was very attractive, bein' at the mouth of the Connecticut River and all. From up on the hill they could hear them Christians just singin' away every night and it was slowly driving old man Mc Clarron crazy. Finally, the old man couldn't stand it no longer, so he made a plan to get rid of these meddlers once and for all. He figured that no one would be brave enough to stand up to his clan once they disposed of them Christians. Mc Clarron decided to burn them out come the next Sunday night while they was singin' and prayin'. He figured that would give those poor people a proper send-off. It didn't much matter that all their children would be there too. Like I said, a nastier bunch never existed. Well, folks, one of the Mc Clarron boys got drunk and spilled the beans to some of the local townsfolk, who of course warned the Christians, hoping to get the Christians to cancel their meeting. That night the Christian folk would have none of it. They posted guards at the door and carried on, just like always. Folks say it was one of the strangest looking nights they'd ever seen. Storm clouds formed all day, but no rain ever came. By nightfall, the moon played hide and seek with the clouds and it was real spooky. The McClarrons had secretly brought in some of the relatives and split up into two parties. The old man and a party of five moved down river while another group of five came in over from the hill. The two groups moved towards each other just up from the south end of the harbor. But before they could strike they heard what sounded like the howling of a wolf. As there were no wolves ever seen in these parts, they just shrugged it off. Once again, they heard the howl of a wolf. The old man was determined to carry out his dastardly deed, so he gave the order to attack. But, over the sounds of the singin' voices of the Christian folks was heard the most god-awful noises. Screams and cries so loud, folks up in Centerview must have heard them. Then guns started firing like crazy, but the crying and the hollering didn't stop. Finally, after some time all the noise ended, and it was as quiet as it had been loud," said Jim, who was speaking in almost a whisper.

Jim looked around to see all the wide-eyed children looking back at him. Then he let out a long howl, 'aaa ooooooh.' The children nearly jumped out of their skins and a few adults also. Then some laughter took place to release the tension.

Once again, Injun Jim looked around and then continued. "When morning came, the townsfolk came out to see what had happened. Those Christians never left their building. What the townsfolk found was a most horrible sight. Ten Mc Clarron men lay dead on the ground, apparently attacked by animals, specifically, wolves. But some had died from gunshot wounds. They probably got so mixed up from their fear that they just started shooting. As there were no dead animal carcasses around, it's believed that they shot and killed some of their own in the hysteria. The Christians insisted that they be the ones to gather up the bodies and take them up the hill to their families. They even offered to help if the Mc Clarron womenfolk needed it. The Mc Clarrons refused their help and took charge of their dead. That night, once again the silence was shattered by one lonely and awful sound of a wolf." Once again, Injun Jim let out a loud howl and once again, the children jumped. "The next day all the Mc Clarrons were gone. They deserted their homestead and left, dead bodies and all. No one knows what happened to them and no one has ever seen or heard a wolf in these parts ever since. The local Indians named this place Wolf Harbor and it's been called that by the locals ever since. By the way, the ground we're standing on is where the Mc Clarrons were attacked."

Some of the young girls in the crowd let out shrieks. Then everyone gave Injun Jim a huge round of applause. Sam stepped forward and invited everyone over to the dinner tent. Injun Jim had provided a great start to the evening.

The festivities ended after ten o'clock. The annual Tyler cookout had been a huge success. Everyone seemed to like the Tylers. Martha made note of this along with the fact that every once in a while during the evening's festivities an uneasy feeling came over her as though she were being watched or stared at. Sure enough, more than once during the course of the evening, her eyes met Alison Tinsley's icy stares.

"Mary was right," she concluded. "This Alison Tinsley is going to bear watching."

CHAPTER 3

July 4th, 1943, was a day of perfect sun filled skies, warm gentle breezes, and an eerie quietness uncharacteristic for the holiday. The town council of Old Saybrook had voted to forego their annual parade out of respect for the war. No one was sure of what the appropriate behavior might be. Certainly, the parading of beauty queens and clowns just didn't seem right to most folks. American flags were on display more this day then anyone ever recalled for Independence Day, or any other day, for that matter.

The congregation at St. John's Episcopal Church, located in the center of Main Street, Essex, finished singing their third hymn and settled into the seats of the magnificent red stone building built by the Hay and Tucker families in 1894. Everyone had come to hear the word from Reverend Linus Foster. The kindly Reverend was in his late sixties. Reverend Foster had a shock of white hair that never seemed to be able to settle into a style. With horn-rimmed glasses just barely clinging to the edges of his nose, the good Reverend slowly made his way to the pulpit. Martha had not brought any Sunday go-to meeting type clothes with her, not that she had any to begin with; Aunt Clara assured her that she looked just fine and proper. One of Aunt Clara's beautiful silk scarves acted as a perfect bonnet. This church thing was a completely new experience for Martha, whose parents were part of the Albany, New York literati. They had no time for spiritual involvement. They believed only in intellect and reason and instilled those noble ideas in their one and only child. Martha thought it strange that she felt so comfortable. She found the music soothing to the soul. It was only that Aunt Clara, Sam, and the children had insisted that she join them for this special July 4th service at church. Martha was glad that they had.

"Thank you all for coming this morning," Reverend Foster began. "We gather today to give special thanks for this wonderful country of ours and to keep all of our fighting boys in our prayers. It is fitting that we carry on in our daily lives just as always, but also let us never forget those who are fighting a terrible war so that we may enjoy such freedoms. Let us pray especially for their loved ones, for they bear the heaviest weight in times like this."

As the Reverend was speaking, Chief Taft made his way quietly up the outside isle and caught Sam's attention. Sam had to excuse himself as the chief obviously had some news.

Sam met the chief on the front steps.

"Sorry to bother you, Sam, but we just got word from the police in New Haven that there were wood fragments in the professor's head; probably from an oar, they suspect."

"That doesn't seem too far-fetched," countered Sam.

"Yeah, but get this," said Chief Taft, "a few of the head wounds were so damaging that they must have been done by a heavy metal object. Now that just seems strange to me."

"That just goes along with my foul mood theory," thought Sam, who kept that thought to himself. Sam knew that his offbeat sense of humor was something that the local police found hard to deal with.

"Do they have any thoughts?" Sam inquired.

"Given the time lines, it appeared that the metal strikes were first. They're sure that the wood strikes came hours later. Either the professor wasn't dead, so the killer finished him off, after moving the body, of course, or there was an attempt to distort the facts and confuse us into thinking the murder happened in the boatyard. The body had been taken to the state's new forensics lab in New Britain. I guess the governor thought this was big stuff. Anyway, the people in New Britain are more equipped for this kind of case," said the chief.

Not surprised by the chief's news, Sam knew that the state's forensics lab was built to investigate crimes such as this.

"Any word on the Griswold guests?" asked Sam.

"Oh yeah," said the chief. "Four out of the six have been cleared. One boarded his train hours before the killing occurred. Another was an eighty-year-old grandmother and the last two are a couple from Michigan, folks who've never been anywhere before coming here. They're on their way to New York City from Montreal, Canada. They only stayed overnight. Their story checks out."

"What about the others?" Sam inquired.

"Well, one seems promising," said the chief. "She's a female baseball player from the women's professional league."

The chief sensed Sam's skepticism.

"Now just hold on, Sam," he said. "The people at the Gris said that this woman actually got into some arm wrestling matches with a few of the male guests to show how strong she was."

"Did she win any?" asked Sam, not really expecting an affirmative answer.

"Yeah," the chief replied. "So it's conceivable that she could have struck the professor and carried him to the boatyard. She certainly is capable of lifting an oar to strike."

In his mind, Sam had already written that suspect off.

"And the other?" he asked.

"A woman professor from Tulane University in Louisiana who's traveled a lot according to the head of her department. But it doesn't appear as though she and the professor have ever crossed paths. No one at the inn remembers them even acknowledging each other. Besides, those who did remember her said that she kept to herself, a real introverted type. You know a scientist. Now Professor Weiss, on the other hand, was a regular one-man show. Folks up at Harvard characterized him as a blowhard, a real intellectual bore. By the way, he wasn't married nor did he seem to have any prospects."

The expression on Sam's face spoke volumes.

"I'll keep you posted," promised the chief as he headed down the steps to his car.

Sam made his way back into the church to join Martha and his family just in time to hear Reverend Foster tell the congregation to enjoy themselves this evening at the town fair.

"Let's not forget," he concluded, "that half of all the moneys collected this evening is going to the war effort, so spend and enjoy."

With that, the service was over. The congregation sang one final hymn, "All is Well With My Soul" and filed out. Lillith took hold of Martha's hand.

Another Tyler tradition was lunch at the Griswold Inn on special days. Sam insisted that Aunt Clara take those days off. Christmas, Easter, and Thanksgiving Day were at home but all other special days were off limits. It was usually lunch or dinner at the Gris. There were a few special times when the Templetons entertained them. They were times especially exciting for the children, as dinner at the Templetons was a grand affair. Sam had no problem with that. The day would come when his children would be adults and extremely wealthy. It only made sense to expose them as much as possible to their maternal grandparents. As far as Sam was concerned, they just didn't come any better than Arlen and Betty Templeton. He deeply appreciated the few years he had spent as their son-in-law. He knew that he was always welcome in their home. In fact, their complaint was that Sam didn't visit more often. It really made him feel special. Sally's death was devastating to all, but to their credit, the Templetons carried on their relationship with Sam as though Sally were still among them. Yes, they just didn't come any better than the Templetons.

The crowd at the Gris was raucous. All the guests in the main dining room knew each other. It was a time for socializing and fellowship. After dining, the men gathered on one side of the room and the women and children on the other. All the women were anxious for Martha to share fashion and society news from New York. The conversation with the men was divided down the middle. Half wanted to talk to Sam about the murder. The other half was more interested in the dark haired beauty from New York staying with Aunt Clara.

Martha sat with Aunt Clara on the back porch, enjoying the warm gentle early evening breezes. It was a pleasurable way to pass the time waiting for Sam and the children to join them. Thomas was the first to emerge from the Tyler home. He was a burst of energy running giddily across Aunt Clara's lawn.

"Well, young man," said Aunt Clara, "where's everybody else?"

"Boy oh boy, Aunt Clara, Mary and Lillith always take so long to get ready," came Thomas's exasperated, half out of breath reply. "I surely don't know what all the fuss is about. It's nighttime, it's not like anyone is going to really see them."

Martha had to laugh. "Someday, Thomas, you'll understand women. Believe me, you'll learn to appreciate them when you get a little older."

Thomas gave Martha a puzzled look. He didn't seem to be convinced.

"Trust me on this. There'll come a day when you'll be grateful that a young lady fusses for you."

Thomas blushed. "Aw shucks, Miss Martha, everybody knows that scientists have no time for women," he informed her.

Martha and Aunt Clara gave each other a knowing glance as Sam and the girls made their way to the porch.

"Tuck your shirt in, Thomas," Mary scolded. "I swear you are such a vagabond."

Sam intervened before Thomas protested. "Come on everybody, we don't want to miss any of the attractions."

Martha and Aunt Clara joined the group and headed up Main Street towards the town park. Aunt Clara walked ahead with the children.

"Are you alright?" Sam asked.

"I'm kind of nervous," Martha confessed. "Aunt Clara tells me there'll be many more people here than the other night. The way she tells it, half of the county will be here."

Sam just gave her a smile and took her hand as they walked. He had already seen the impact Martha had made on the locals. The older women thought she was great, sharing all the juicy gossip about New York, while the younger women were appearing to be quite threatened by this big city beauty who had thrust herself, completely uninvited, into their midst. The obvious interest of the young men was adding to the cause for concern. One thing is for sure; there would be many short leashes enforced this evening.

The carnival atmosphere seemed more alive than in years, providing a welcome release from tense times. The war had a sobering impact on everyone. News of the war effort was usually days behind so it was hard for the people to respond to anything. The German tank division had assaulted Africa and would ultimately be facing General Patton's forces. Under the leadership of Field Marshall Rommell, who had earned the nickname the "Desert Fox," the Germans were a formidable force. Japan was engaged in the Pacific, the Germans bogged down in Russia, and Italy under Mussolini was another front helping to spread out the ranks of the allied forces. France had fallen but the French Resistance was causing havoc for the occupation forces. Evidence of genocide of the Jews in Germany was beginning to substantiate the worst fears of the free world. There was also talk of atrocities carried out by the Japanese on the Chinese mainland. It seemed as though half of the world had gone mad. How all this horror and evil existed in these modern times was causing shock and disbelief for the other half.

Yes, the carnival gave the people some much-needed relief.

Aunt Clara and Martha took the children in tow while Sam made himself available to the local businessmen and elected officials. Everyone wanted to know how the investigation was going. Murder was something that never happened in Essex. No one knew how to deal with it. They generally agreed that there was no reason to suspect any harm for the local population, but murder was never good for any community. Businesses were slow due to the war, and the summer tourist season was down considerably for the same reason. It was a well-established fact that the area didn't need any more problems than it already had.

Sam tried to assure everyone that the local and state police were working as fast as they could to end this difficult situation. By the time he made his way back to the family, it was evident that Thomas had exceeded his sugar tolerance level. Sam gave Aunt Clara a wary look as he picked cotton candy from Thomas's hair.

"I'm afraid that this is my fault," said Martha. "Thomas felt that I was paying too much attention to the girls so I kind of overindulged him. Please don't be mad."

Sam just paused there for a moment to gather his thoughts. "Let's all stick together for a while," he proposed.

This pleased the children. Mary, of course, had to make a comment concerning Thomas's gluttony, while Lillith made a comment concerning Mary's comment. It was a typical evening with the Tyler family.

The family walked over to the arena for pony rides to see Injun Jim. Injun Jim was whooping it up for the toddlers taking their first ride. Of course, Aunt Clara had something to say concerning Injun Jim; she always did. "A full blooded American Indian who's never been on a horse is giving pony rides to the local children. You've got to admit that Injun Jim is a real piece of work."

Martha had to laugh. Aunt Clara was a feisty woman, which was for sure. Poor Injun Jim never stood a chance with her, but in spite of all her nagging Injun Jim was loyal to a fault where Aunt Clara was concerned.

"Sam, Sam Tyler," came the booming words from Mayor Tinsley, "come on over here, son."

Sam turned to see. The mayor and his family were standing just a few feet away with a man Sam had never met.

"Give me a few minutes," Sam said.

"Go pay your respects to the old blowhard," barked Aunt Clara. "Just don't get too close to that daughter of his." Aunt Clara refused to call Allison Tinsley by name. "She looks extra hungry tonight."

Martha was both shocked and amused by Aunt Clara's words. Any doubts she may have had concerning her had been forever dispelled by Aunt Clara's stinging remarks. It was clear to Martha that she loved this woman.

It took almost half an hour to pull himself away from the mayor whose guest was the new State's Attorney General James Buckley. Sam and Mr. Buckley seemed to make a connection. They agreed to meet in Hartford so Sam could bring the attorney general up to snuff concerning the Professor Weiss homicide. The murder of the professor from Harvard had the attorney general more than a little anxious. Sam sensed Mr. Buckley's genuine concern and concluded that this new attorney general might turn out to be a valuable ally.

Allison Tinsley did her best to make an impact on Sam, but Sam was able to gracefully sidestep her advances and pull himself away. He started to make his way through the crowd when he spotted Martha standing alone in front of the coffee and dessert stand. Martha was halfway through a coffee, black, and no sugar.

"Where is everybody?" asked Sam.

"Over by the gazebo," said Martha. "I think the children are getting tired."

"Come on, let's walk," said Sam.

Sam and Martha walked for a while in silence down to the waters of the inner bay.

"You're quiet," he said.

Martha finished her coffee and placed her empty cup in a trashcan, but said nothing.

"There's something wrong, isn't there?" he inquired.

Martha hesitated for a second then said, "That Allison Tinsley really has a thing for you. She's an attractive lady. How is it that you two have not connected?"

At first Sam smiled, but then he took hold of both of Martha's arms and turned serious.

Martha looked up into Sam's eyes while hers seemed to grow even larger. Sam had to admit, he really liked looking into those eyes.

"Well," answered Sam, "you might say that she's just not my type. And besides as far as looks go, that lady could never hold a candle to you," he said.

That took Martha totally by surprise. Sam drew her closer; she did not resist.

"There you are," called out Mary. "For goodness sake, we've been looking all over for you two."

Sam gently released Martha and turned to acknowledge his oldest daughter. A tender moment had been interrupted, but that did not change the fact that a statement had been made. As far as Sam was concerned, Martha would be gone by summer's end and possibly even sooner, but he was not about to deny that for the first time in years he felt something really good. In all probability, there was little chance for a future between two people from such vastly different worlds, but Sam wasn't going to pull back. He had sent a clear message: one that Martha could not miss.

Martha wearily climbed the stairs to her quarters. A thousand thoughts were running through her mind. There was no mistaking what had happened or almost happened with Sam. She quickly washed her face to remove her makeup, something she never omitted no matter how tired she was. That attention to detail showed in her flawless complexion, one that was the envy of most women. Martha always sensed their silent jealousy. A sumptuous head of flowing auburn hair and a gorgeous complexion, now that was sure to win Martha many female friends along the way. Martha somewhat enjoyed the whole idea.

As she lay in bed, she couldn't shake the feeling of Sam's strong, muscular body against hers. It lasted only a few seconds, but the weakness in her legs, her total inability to resist both concerned and intrigued her. There was no denying that Sam was what the girls back in New York called a man's man, one vastly different from the corporate or literary types Martha was surrounded by in her world. "The gals in New York would fall all over themselves for someone like Sam," she mused. But the dilemma was too obvious to dismiss. She was big city and Sam was not. Her life was totally hers, such as it was. She came and went as she pleased with no restrictions placed on her. Sam's, on the other hand, was a life of duty, of family, of responsibilities. He couldn't just come and go as he pleased. He had a wonderful family that needed him, counted on him. Martha started to realize that she might be losing her own argument. Nevertheless, she was darn sure that she wouldn't allow herself too many moments alone with Sam Tyler. Who knows, maybe he might enjoy indulging himself in a little summer fling, but Martha was not going to cast herself as the odd person out in any love drama. With that thought clearly settled in her mind, Martha dozed off.

CHAPTER 4

Aunt Clara told Sam that Mary and Thomas had gone up to Zuckerman's. Lillith and Martha were taking a walk up on the hill. Sam pulled his cruiser in front of Zuckerman's and went in. The local hangout was all abuzz over the story in the New Haven Register concerning radio signals apparently coming from somewhere in the Essex, Saybrook area. The code used was not one familiar to the Coast Guard that picked them up off Montauk Point, Long Island. Some of the local old-timers were sitting around, expounding on as many possible scenarios as they could dream up.

"It can't be the Japanese," said one. "They're too far away."

"Now that's just plain stupid," said another. "Of course they're too far away, even a fool knows that."

"Well that's what I said," protested the first.

"Why even bring up the Japanese?" chimed in a third. "It would be hard enough for the Germans to get this close. Maybe the Italians found a fishing boat that could make the trip," he mocked. "Can those damn Italians even afford a Navy?"

Sam walked in just in time to see Nate Zuckerman burying his head in his hands. Thomas and Mary were sitting at the counter drinking their strawberry floats.

"Thank God you're here, Sam," said Nate. "I was getting concerned for your children, here, listening to all this nonsense going on."

Before Sam responded, the three older men began stating their cases. As things heated up, Sam looked over to the children who were obviously fascinated by the whole experience. Children rarely permitted to be present when adults carried on heated discussions were totally enjoying themselves.

Finally, one man blurted out, "Well, how about the report in the New York Times a few weeks back about the mysterious radio signals coming from Montauk? What do you two geniuses make of that?" he questioned.

For a moment, there was silence, but then Thomas broke the silence.

"If someone was transmitting from here to Montauk, it makes perfect sense that someone there might be transmitting from a tanker going out of Brooklyn, New York across the Atlantic."

Again, there was silence. "Well, it could happen," protested Thomas.

Once again, the men began jabbering away. They had to admit, Thomas's argument had merit.

"That's one smart son you have there, Sam," said Nate Zuckerman.

No one seemed to be able to refute Thomas's theory, something that pleased Thomas no end. Mary, of course, had a real problem on these occasions as she just expected that she, being the oldest, would be the originator of all words of wisdom. Though both children were at the top of their respective classes in school, Thomas possessed a keen mind, far beyond his years. Sam was too busy churning this scenario over in his mind to acknowledge Thomas's revelation. Mary was proud of her brother, but it didn't take away the sting of seeing Thomas standing alone in the limelight.

Just then, Martha and Lillith came through the door. Sam greeted them and then bid a hasty goodbye. He got into the cruiser and made his way through town heading to the barracks in Westbrook. He put in a call to Chief Taft over in Old Saybrook.

"Round up the names of every ham operator in the area," he ordered the chief. "See if you can get a name for any amateur radio operator in the area."

"You got something?" asked the chief.

"I'm not sure," said Sam. "Did you read about the radio signals off Montauk in the Register?" he inquired.

"Yeah, you think that has something to do with our case?"

"Normally, I'd have to say that I wouldn't give it a second thought as far as we're concerned. But when you figure where we sit, between Yale, Pratt Reed and Groton, I don't know. It seems the death of our Harvard professor has international implications. It's still sketchy in my mind, but I can't shake this gut feeling," said Sam.

"Always go with the gut, Sam," said the chief. "I'll see what I can come up with for you. Some of the boys down at the station house are into that ham radio stuff. These types usually know one another pretty good. I'll keep you posted."

Sam signed off and headed towards the Clinton barracks.

Dinner at Aunt Clara's was a welcome relief for Sam, whose day was anything but eventful. Chief Taft was busy compiling a list of amateur radio operators in the area, while Sam was busy watching the paint age on the walls of the barracks. It had been that kind of a day.

"Well," said Aunt Clara, "seems as though Master Thomas caused quite a stir over at Zuckerman's today."

Thomas was beaming. The whole town seemed to be talking about Thomas's exposure of a major sabotage conspiracy, carried out right in their own back yard.

"Well, let's just hope that Thomas's head doesn't get so big that it topples off his shoulders," cautioned Mary.

Lillith quickly came to Thomas's defense. "Oh, Thomas," she exclaimed, "we're all so proud of you. My big brother sure showed those old geezers a thing or two."

"Old geezers?" questioned Sam. "Where did you learn that saying, young lady?" Sam demanded.

Lillith lowered her head and turned slightly in the direction of Aunt Clara. Martha put her hands over her face trying to conceal her laugh. Sam sat back in his chair and directed his attention towards his aunt.

"Well, you've really done yourself proud this time, Auntie dear," he scolded. "Is there anything else I should be concerned about?" he asked her.

"Oh, Aunt Clara teaches us all kinds of neat things to say," piped Thomas.

"Oh, Thomas," said Mary.

"What," asked Thomas? "What did I say? I didn't say anything wrong."

"That will be quite enough, Samuel Tyler," announced Aunt Clara. "I believe you've had just about enough fun at my expense."

Before Sam said anything, the telephone rang. Aunt Clara went to the hall, answered it, and told Sam it was for him.

"We'll finish our conversation later," Sam informed Aunt Clara.

"What?" yelled Sam into the phone, not believing what Chief Taft had just told him? "I'll be right there."

Sam dropped the phone and headed back into the kitchen.

"Robert Rucker has just been arrested for the murder of Professor Weiss," he told the stunned family. "They got an anonymous tip from someone and found the professor's wallet and some personal items stuffed in Robert's car.

I'll call you from the station when I know more," he said, running out the back door.

Aunt Clara said nothing but went back into the hall and picked up the phone. She dialed the Rucker household and soon learned that the Ruckers were aware of Robert's arrest.

"Don't you believe a word of it," she instructed Marvin Rucker. "You people sit tight, I'll be right over."

Marvin tried to protest, but the line had already gone dead. Aunt Clara was on the way.

"Could you please stay with the children?" she asked Martha. "Ella Mae will need me. That darn son of hers has gotten into trouble again."

"You go right ahead, the children and I will be just fine," Martha assured Aunt Clara.

Next, Aunt Clara called Injun Jim. "I need you to take me over to the Rucker's," she said. "That's right, right now. Do you think I'd call now if I meant tomorrow?" she asked. She didn't wait for an answer. "You can find the Rucker's home in the dark, can't you?" she demanded. "Good, well, get right over here then, mister," she ordered.

Aunt Clara hung up the telephone and headed to her room to get a shawl. "Damn Indian couldn't find snow in a blizzard," she exclaimed. Aunt Clara came off as feisty, but inside, her heart was aching for Ella Mae.

Robert Rucker was a sorry sight. He was sitting in the interrogation room all hunched over and shaking uncontrollably.

"I'm innocent, Sam," Robert yelled out as Sam Tyler entered the room. The outer offices were running over with police, members of the town council and even Mayor Tinsley. Things didn't look good for Robert right now.

"Yeah, he's innocent as a newborn babe," said Chief Taft. "Just look at him, Sam, half drunk as usual. And guess what, he can't account for his whereabouts on the murder night."

Sam walked over, drew up a chair, and sat down next to Rucker. He looked Robert straight in the eyes and asked, "Did you do it, Robert?"

"No sir, no I did not," said Rucker.

"Robert," Sam said, still looking him in the eyes. "Are you one hundred percent sure? No doubts, no questions?"

"I'm sure, Sam, as God is my witness, I'm sure. Sure, I'm a drunk and a screw-up, but dear Lord, I ain't no murderer. No way I'm capable of that," he pleaded.

The door to the interrogation room opened and Jefferson Fine, the county prosecutor, entered.

"Does he have an attorney?" Fine asked.

"I just spoke to his father and he said that they are trying to contact one now," said the chief.

"No more questions till this man gets an attorney," said Fine.

Sam got up, patted Rucker on the shoulder, and said, "I'll be back, Robert. For your mother's sake, I hope you are being honest here."

"Oh Sam, I'm really sorry. I know this looks bad but I swear, I'd never do nothing to cause my momma such shame."

"Alright, Robert," Sam said. "Let's see if we can get to the truth here. I'll be back in the morning."

With that, Sam and the chief left the interrogation room. "You don't look too pleased," said the chief.

"Nothing's ever this easy," said Sam. "Any idea who tipped you guys off?"

"We just figured that it was one of the bums he hangs around with. Who knows, maybe he got somebody mad or maybe a murder made someone nervous," said the chief.

"I don't know," said Sam. "I've known Robert for a lot of years. I'm not saying he couldn't kill someone, but to do it twice feels like the act of a truly desperate person. Given Robert's usual state, I just don't think he's capable of doing it twice; that takes more than desperation or even fear."

"Well, you may be right, Sam, but right now he's what we've got. Buckley has political aspirations and a case like this could really help his cause. Besides, Buckley is a barracuda. He smells fear and knows how to go for the kill. I know Rucker's momma works for you, Sam, so you'd better make sure that the attorney they get is the best. Believe me, they'll need it."

"I'll call Arlen. I'm sure he'll know who to call. Talk to you later, Ethan," said Sam.

Sam called the Rucker household and told them he was on his way over. When he got there, he told Injun Jim to go back home to stay with Martha and the children. Sam would take Aunt Clara home. All the Rucker children were there with their families. It was good to see such a show of family unity.

"Any luck with an attorney?" Sam asked Marvin.

"Not really, Sam. We got some calls in to our friends, but Aunt Clara told us we should wait on you, so we did."

"Good," said Sam. "I'll call Arlen Templeton if that's alright with you."

Marvin looked to his wife Ella Mae who nodded yes.

"Can I use your phone?" Sam requested.

Marvin pointed it out.

Sam called his ex-father-in-law and explained the situation. Arlen, in turn, took the Rucker's phone number and then called Carlton Weimer in Hartford. Weimer was widely considered the premier defense attorney in Connecticut. He was an eccentric who lived in a thirty-room castle on the Connecticut River in Glastonbury, south of Hartford. The great attorney had a license to practice law in Massachusetts, Rhode Island, and New York. Few attorneys ventured beyond the boundaries and legal system of their home state, but Carlton Weimer was a man who lived large and played even larger. From the "Cottages" of Newport to the "Castles" on the Hudson, Weimer was a player to be reckoned with. As fate would have it, Weiner had just turned fifty-five years old and had decided to do more playing and less practicing. With two sons and a daughter who were a major part of his law firm, Weimer was in a position to do his old friend a favor. Twenty-five years ago, Arlen Templeton had talked Weimer into a business deal that over the years made him an enormously rich man. With wealth on his side, the brilliant Weimer literally conquered the state. Many of the great families of Greenwich called him friend and now one in Essex was calling.

Marvin Rucker handed the phone to Sam who stood in total disbelief as Arlen Templeton explained that Carlton Weiner himself would be at the Old Saybrook Police headquarters at eleven a.m. tomorrow. The Ruckers were ecstatic with the news. Now their ne'er-do-well son had a fighting chance.

Sam and Aunt Clara said their goodbyes and began to leave. Marvin Rucker escorted them onto the front porch.

"How can we ever thank you, Sam? We owe you so much already," he said.

"Let's just hope for the best, Marvin. Let's pray that Robert is innocent. At least now we can be sure that the county prosecutor won't be able to railroad him," said Sam. "He'll get a fair deal, you can be sure of that."

"And if my son is guilty?" asked Marvin with a painful look in his eyes.

His question caught Sam totally off guard. An awkward moment played out in silence. Sam just shrugged, he knew, but couldn't say.

"We Ruckers are Christians, Sam. That means that we don't take a life unless it's in self-defense. Because Robby is my son does not release me from my beliefs. If Robby is guilty, all we can hope for is . . ." Marvin couldn't finish the sentence. It was too heavy a weight to bear.

"Let's just wait and see," said Sam. "If it helps, I just don't think Robert had anything to do with this. Call it a hunch, but I think that there is much more here than an out of work townie murdering a tourist. Just keep the faith and maybe you and your family can say some prayers to aid me in my investigation. The sooner I find out some things the sooner Robert's cleared. I really believe that. As for now, Robert is in good hands."

Marvin looked heavenward and said, "I know Sam, I know."

All the way home Aunt Clara asked Sam what seemed like a million questions. Sam understood. Aunt Clara was devoted to Ella Mae and her family.

"That fool son has caused those people so much pain," said Aunt Clara, angrily.

"Well, until I can come up with some answers, they're going to feel a lot more. You can bet the county prosecutor is going to drag Robert Rucker's life through the mud. He won't be far wrong, no matter what he says. That's going to be hard for the Ruckers to swallow. I've got to work fast."

"Yes, you do," said Aunt Clara with conviction.

"How ironic," Sam thought to himself, "A perfectly lousy ending to a perfectly lousy day."

Sam drove down the slate stone covered driveway of 21 West Main Street, the home of Arlen and Betty Templeton. He parked in front of the four-car garage then walked to the side door and rang the bell. Within seconds, the Templeton's maid greeted him and led him to Arlen's study.

"Sam, my boy," came the warm, bellowing greeting from the master of the house. "You're just in time for breakfast."

"I'm sorry to intrude, sir," said Sam. "I thought you ate breakfast much earlier."

"That's true, but today I had to deal with some things that needed my immediate attention. I decided to wait till all that was out of the way so we could enjoy our breakfast in the solarium. Come, join us, it's beautiful out there this time of morning," said Templeton.

Betty Templeton rose when she saw Sam and came quickly over to give him a hug; no faux kisses to each side of the cheek for the man she still considered her son-in-law. "Kisses to the wind" is what she called those appalling gestures. Betty was an Irish beauty, one of the three well-bred daughters of the Murpheys of Boston, Newport, and Hyannis. Sam always thought of Betty as an older version of his Sally. She was well preserved and unbelievably normal for one from such a moneyed clan. Betty's father, the famous Massachusetts political boss John Murphy, took a dim view of his daughter's uncultured choice. It was only after Arlen informed him that he would become so successful one day that he'd buy Murphy, sell him at a loss, and still make a profit that the great man was completely won over. Murphy lived to see those words come true, such was the wealth amassed by the brazen Templeton.

Every meal at the Templeton's was an event and this impromptu shift in scheduling was no exception. The finest china, silverware, chafing dishes and the like, extravagant by most people's standards, were just simple everyday dining for Arlen and Betty.

The group spent the time discussing the children until breakfast was complete. Betty then excused herself to leave the men to their business.

"Well, Sam, what's on your mind?" Templeton asked.

"I just wanted to ask you how to approach Carlton Weimer about his fee," said Sam. "The Ruckers couldn't possibly afford someone like Carlton Weimer. I'd like to pay that bill and get an idea of what that number might be."

"Sam, Sam, don't be so serious," said Arlen. "Do you really think I would involve someone like Carlton in this matter if there was a fee attached?"

Sam was confused.

"Old Weimer owes me more favors than he can count. It would take two lifetimes for him to catch up. Consider the matter closed, Sam, there won't be any bills coming in the mail."

"But, sir," Sam tried to protest.

Arlen cut him off. "My wife adores you, Sam, you know that. She'd skin me alive if I didn't do this for you. I gotta tell you, I really admire you for taking up that family's cause. Betty and I are just grateful that you feel comfortable enough to call on us at a time like this. It makes us feel like we are still part of your life. I know that the children bind us, but we'd both like you to know that you will always be a part of our lives even if you should remarry."

It was good to hear how the Templetons felt towards him, but that last remark about remarrying; did Arlen suspect something?

"I was on the phone to Washington this morning. Looks like our boys are doing alright over there. The tide is slowly turning. You just have to know what to look for. Patton is about to engage Rommell in Africa. The Germans have never met anyone like George Patton. That Rommell fellow is a real genius, but Patton is a giant. He is so much larger than life. You'll see, they're in for a big surprise. Old George is about to cook their goose, real good. And Mac-Arthur, well, what can you say about him? The Nazis and the Japanese simply don't have enough fighting people to sustain a prolonged war with us and the allies. Besides, our war machinery is growing while theirs is dwindling. It's a shame so many of our people will have to suffer and die before this thing is over, but you mark my words, the outcome is inevitable. Neither Germany nor Japan ever imagined that the rest of the world would rise up as we have. And the Italian people never wanted any part of this, that fool Mussolini dragged those poor bastards into this. The Italians' day came and went with the Romans. It's been almost two thousand years for them. Too bad the Italians will have to suffer for the sake of one egomaniac."

Arlen's vast knowledge of what was going on in the world impressed Sam.

"Wait here, I want to show you something," said Arlen, excusing himself. Moments later he reappeared and placed a picture in front of Sam; the picture showed a small, neatly landscaped home.

"What's this?" asked Sam.

"The future," said Arlen.

Once again, Sam was confused.

"This house is a whole new idea. We got the concept from the manufacturing of our gliders over in Deep River. They're modular, Sam, prefabricated, pre-built. The house comes ready made in sections built in a factory, shipped to its destination, and put up in a fraction of the time it takes to build one from scratch. After the war, our population is going to explode. There'll be so many families being started that there won't be anywhere for these people to live. The market will never be able to keep up, unless we are prepared."

"And you have a plan?" asked Sam.

"You bet your life, son. A group of money people, Weimer included, has been buying up large parcels of land in the Northeast and California. We're going to develop a new idea called planned communities. And what we need to make the whole thing work is affordable housing. So everyone who wants one will be able to afford one. All they have to do is make a small down payment and the banks will lend them the rest. Of course the banks stand to make a lot of money over the years."

"Of course," offered Sam. "And you and your people have large interests in . . . ."

"The banks," Arlen completed the sentence.

"Sounds good," said Sam. "The rich really do get richer, don't they?"

"Yes, they do," said Templeton, "but let's not forget that the rich often get that way from planning and then taking all the risks. If they fail, it's doom."

"And will they fail?" Sam asked with a knowing smile on his face.

"Not a chance," said a confident and rich Arlen Templeton.

Sam walked to his car, his thoughts drifting back to a happier time. He and Sally visited her parents almost daily when she was pregnant with Mary. Those were good times and life was special. Since Sally's passing, only the kids and his work kept Sam going.

As Sam drove away the answer to the question of Arlen's confidence in the war's outcome kept playing over in his mind. "I spent some time in Germany and dealt with the Nazi régime before Hitler got so crazy. I think I know these people, Sam, and believe me, they are no match for us and the British. I don't believe they have the stomach for the defeats they are experiencing. Hitler sold them on the idea of invincibility. I guess that theory went out the window. And Hirohito, I believe he knows the mistake he made. I'm sure that if he could take Pearl Harbor back, he wouldn't hesitate; especially when he sees our rebuilt fleet squeezing the life from his and Germany's Nazis."

Arlen Templeton possessed a vast knowledge of classified information. His extensive contacts in the state and federal governments, carefully acquired over the years, had served him well. Arlen's father had schooled him in the art of playing politics. Old man Templeton had taught Arlen the fundamental facts that politicians come and go; the product of a fickle public. But those on the outside with staying power, and a little useful knowledge could apply the principles of special interests when dealing with those who would welcome any means to prolong their career in office.

Arlen knew much more than he was letting on to Sam, but he really cared for the husband of his deceased daughter. He wanted to assure Sam that America very definitely had begun to turn the tide of the war in its favor. Allied intelligence learned that certain Nazi generals, Rommel included, were becoming increasingly hostile over Hitler's failing attempts to run their military campaign; something he had no previous knowledge or experience in doing. An unsuccessful attempt on Hitler's life had rendered the "Fuhrer" paralyzed in a state of hysterical paranoia. Rommel received an order to go back to Germany for an audience with Hitler, who up to now had no real idea as to the identity of the impending assassins. That move would prove to be fatal.

By late August, Patton would have clobbered the Germans in the Tunisian desert during the battle of El Guettar, Rommel's forces, in his absence, would be dealt a crushing defeat at Mortian, the result being the once fierce panzer division would be decimated and rendered useless. Hitler's aggressive Atlantic Wall Campaign, which was the lynchpin for his success in Western Europe, was doomed to failure due to Rommel's inability to muster enough forces to come to its aid.

The success of the D Day landings and the allied push through France were glaring evidence of how critical that Atlantic Wall was in guarding Germany's western frontier. Later Rommel sustained a wound by a crack Canadian spitfire ace, thus taking him out of the action. Later on, a crazed and desperate Hitler had Rommel killed, an act that sealed his own fate; no German general felt safe from the Fuhrer's wrath. Those loyal to Germany would carry on at their own peril. Those who were more interested in saving their own hides would look for opportunities to kill Hitler. And the sooner the better.

None of this would surprise Arlen Templeton, who had the amazing ability to look at all circumstances like pieces of a puzzle. Arlen's main concern was to work every angle to produce a successful conclusion for himself and those who were in league with him. By the end of the war, Arlen and his partners would be poised to supply an anxious American public with sufficient housing for the coming postwar boom.

But as for now Sam was going to have to carry on his attempts to solve a case, which up to now was not providing anything in the way of clues. Then there was the slight problem of Robert Rucker. Sam was hoping for any information, no matter how small, to offer a glimmer of hope where Rucker's innocence was concerned. Sam knew how much the Ruckers meant to Aunt Clara, and he sure wasn't thrilled with the likely prospect that he would let her down.

Sam shook the bony, almost gnarled hand of Carlton Weimer, the most feared defense attorney in the state. Sam had seen Weimer's picture many times in the newspapers over the years. He just wasn't ready for the five foot five inch little man standing before him. Sam took quick note that the rest of those present at the police station were treating Carlton Weimer as if he were nine feet tall. The city officials and the local police were falling all over themselves to satisfy Weimer's every request.

"I got here earlier than anticipated and I've already spoken with my client," Weimer said.

"I can't thank you enough, Mr. Weimer," said Sam. "His parents are wonderful people. I have to tell you that my concern was more for them than for Robert's welfare. However, if it means anything, I don't believe that Robert did this."

"Hold that thought, Captain, but it really doesn't matter," said Weimer.

"What do you mean?" asked Sam.

Carlton Weimer led Sam to a corner of the room. "At best, we have circumstantial evidence. They don't have Mr. Rucker's prints on a murder weapon and when my people have a chance to investigate, I'm sure we'll have enough to cast reasonable doubt on the state's case. Trust me, Captain, even if they had his prints, I'd blow so many holes in their case you'd be able to float a barge through it. Now don't you worry, the state has never seen the light of day on a case they could win where Carlton Weimer is involved. By the way, you must mean a lot to Arlen Templeton. He really didn't give me much choice but to accept this case. I'll have you know that I'm missing a fishing trip off the coast of Cuba. Few people could make me do that. Havana's quite the place."

With that, Weimer turned and was gone.

Sam spent some time with Chief Taft. They went over a list of all amateur radio people in the area, looking for a lead. Running background checks and talking to these people would be time consuming, given the small number of police available. The chief asked the police departments of the neighboring towns to lend a hand. Everything takes time, no way around it. The chief also contacted people in Groton and New London where the submarines and naval personnel were located. The question was, did anybody have any ties to Essex or Saybrook? There was no question as to where the signals came from. The trick was to link somebody to those locations.

"Everybody fishes in these parts, Sam, and there sure are a lot of boats," said Nathan Zuckerman. "Anybody could go out at night to send signals and no one would be the wiser."

Sam met Martha and the children for lunch at Zuckerman's. Lunch there usually meant ice cream for the younger Tylers. Zuckerman made his own ice cream, a tradition handed down for many years by his father and grandfather.

Sam knew that what Nate said was true; still, he had no choice but to keep searching for clues.

"Things aren't looking too good, are they?" questioned Martha.

"Well, if you mean that so far we've got nothing, then I guess you're right," Sam retorted.

They looked into each other's eyes for a brief moment and then realized that the children had stopped eating and were staring at them.

"What are you guys doing this afternoon?" asked Sam, breaking the spell.

"Injun Jim is taking us sailing off Essex Island," said Thomas "We'll probably head up river to show Martha the sights," said Mary. "Aunt Clara is packing sandwiches. She guessed that we'd need them after lunch with you, Dad."

Lillith began to giggle. "Aunt Clara's pretty smart, isn't she?" she asked her father.

"Too smart if you ask me," said Sam.

Nathan came out of the office and called to Sam. "Chief Taft's on the line. He needs to speak to you."

"The boys found a metal pipe around back of Rucker's place, Sam. Looks like there's dried blood on it. We've sent it over to Meriden for testing, should know something in a couple of days, so no sense saying anything until we know. I just called Robert's attorney. He was not happy to hear from me."

"I'll bet," said Sam, not convinced by Weimer's bravado, but then again, the man was nearly invincible in a courtroom. Sam chalked it up to Weimer's considering this bit of news more of an aggravation than cause for concern.

"See you for dinner?" asked Martha.

Sam nodded affirmatively. He only half seemed to be there. He walked out, then poked his head back in the door to say goodbye to the children.

"What if the pipe is the murder weapon and Robert's prints are on it?" Sam asked himself. Sure, Weimer could probably get him off, but the Ruckers would never get over the shame. They simply were not the type of people to live with the knowledge that their son had taken someone's life. Sam's load was getting heavier. Things were piling up against Robert and Sam had to work overtime to try to get at what he believed was the truth. The truth, however, was sure playing a mean game of hide and seek.

"Okay, let's have it," said Sam when he heard Chief Taft's voice on the phone back at the barracks.

"Sorry to have to tell you this, Sam, but they found two of Robert's prints on the pipes. At least eleven points matched up. They're almost sure that the pipe is the murder weapon. Like I said, it will take some time before they can really confirm the blood types, but early indications are that they match. It looks real bad for Rucker," said the chief.

Sam just shrugged, took a deep breath, and then let all the air out.

"What am I going to say to the Ruckers?" he asked himself.

As he quite expected, the news devastated the Ruckers. The police were feeling confident that they had the murderer of Professor Weiss in custody. The Ruckers spent the evening with their pastor and closest friends in prayer at the First Baptist Church. Sam had to go home and face Aunt Clara; something that was becoming increasingly hard to do. He had no choice but to tell her about the police discovery.

Aunt Clara took hold of Sam's arms and said "Don't be too hard on yourself, son. I know you're doing everything you can. Sometimes there's just no wishing away the truth. It looks like Robert went too far this time, and his momma and family are going to pay dearly for it. Thank you for doing all that you could, Sam. I'm real proud of you."

"Fingerprints on a murder weapon can be explained away," Sam told his aunt. "I just have this feeling that there is a whole lot we don't know yet. How convenient for us that Robert left the pipe nearby, don't you think? Just how drunk do you have to be to forget where you left that pipe? Then again, what happened to the first weapon? Let's see, you knock somebody unconscious, take them to another place, kill them, go home, drop the pipe behind the building and completely forget about it? Now don't you think that Robert's attorney will ask these questions and more? Don't throw the towel in yet, dear Aunt, we're down, but we're not out."

"Thank you, Sam," said Aunt Clara, "for giving us hope. I'm going up to the First Baptist to pray with the Ruckers. Why don't you take Martha and the children over to Wanda's place? I just didn't feel up to cooking tonight. Anyway, we had a real nice time up river this afternoon and everybody's tired."

Injun Jim took Aunt Clara to be with the Ruckers. Sam took Martha and the children to the Black Swan for dinner. Wanda Loomis was happy to see them and made a big fuss over the children. Later, Sam put the kids to bed and sat with Martha on the patio behind his home.

The two sat in silence for a while, content to look up at the star filled sky and enjoy the warm summer breezes blowing in from the harbor.

"Sam," said Martha finally, "I heard what you said to Aunt Clara and, well, I hope you don't mind, but I drew the same conclusions. To write my stories I've had to spend many hours with the New York Police who have been especially kind to me, allowing me to observe and ask questions. A lieutenant at the third precinct has helped a lot."

"And you worked very closely with him?" queried Sam.

"As close as one might work with one's father," countered Martha.

"You were about to say?" said Sam.

"I don't want to step on any toes, but I do have some thoughts concerning this case. Besides, I'm seriously entertaining the idea of turning it into a book. Would that bother you?"

"Does that mean that you're staying until the case is solved?" asked Sam.

"Oh, that's very good," said Martha.

"You were going to ask something, I think," said Sam.

"Would you be offended if I put my two cents in, just with you, of course? You never know, I might be of some assistance," said Martha.

"You're not thinking of snooping around, are you?" asked Sam.

"Is that a problem?" asked Martha.

"You're damn right it is. Listen here, lady; I think that there is far more to this case than a simple homicide. Don't ask me why, but my instincts tell me that this is serious business and that Robert Rucker is playing the fall guy right now. If I'm right, this could be dangerous. I really don't like the idea of you placing yourself in danger," said Sam.

"And why is that?" asked Martha, directly.

Sam hesitated for a second, unsure of what he should say.

"You're our guest," he stammered, finally. "You came here to rest, not put yourself in jeopardy. We'd never forgive ourselves if something happened to you. And Cousin Ellen would have my head," he said.

"Well, how about if you discussed the case with me and I gave you my input? Can you live with that?" Martha asked.

"No funny business?" countered Sam.

"Honest Injun," said Martha.

"Deal," said Sam stretching out his hand for a handshake. Martha placed her hand in his and they shook on it, but Sam did not release hers.

"I love being here, Sam," said Martha, surprising herself as much as Sam. "I've found so much more here than I ever thought possible, than I ever expected."

"We love having you here," said Sam. "I love having you here."

There was a long pause.

"It probably won't be long before you'll be heading back to New York, but I want you to know that you've made quite an impact on all of us. We're all going to miss you. I've never seen my family take to anyone like they've taken to you. Only a special person could do that."

The telephone rang in the house, breaking the spell.

"I've got to answer that, it might be business," said Sam reluctantly releasing Martha's hand and heading into the house.

"It's just Aunt Clara wondering how we're doing," reported Sam, after a few moments absence. "Come on, I'll walk you over."

Sam and Martha walked across the great lawn in silence, but allowed their bodies to brush up against each other's. This night ended up much nicer than the last.

Chief Taft went down to New Haven on police business while Sam spent the day talking to the military about the radio signals. The Coast Guard was sure that the code was of foreign origin so they called the FBI for help and even notified the president. Word had come down from the oval office to treat this matter seriously.

Sam spent the next day in Hartford with the new state's attorney. James Buckley was impressed with Sam and arranged lunch with the governor for the two of them. The governor was receptive to Sam's theory that the murder in Essex might be much more than meets the eye. Mysterious radio signals off the sound, the death of a high profile Harvard professor who was heading to Yale for a clandestine meeting with some of its exalted chemistry professors, submarines in Groton, experimental gliders in Deep River, too many circumstances to overlook.

The governor readily agreed.

"This wouldn't be the first time the federal government has carried on these kinds of activities right in our own backyard. I realize the need for secrecy where national security is concerned, but dammit, it doesn't make it easier to swallow when things go wrong. Of course, I could call the President, but let's face it, he'd just waltz me around the block. I understand it, but I still don't like it."

"Maybe we're jumping the gun just a little," said the attorney general.

"Oh really," said the governor, impatiently. "I'd like you to know that I got a call from Carlton Weimer yesterday and he expressed many of the same ideas that the captain here has. Weimer has his people all over this and he's coming up with the same conclusions. Why do you think I was so available for lunch? No offense Captain, but this is serious business on a state and national level. I can assure you, sir, that I'm not the one who's going to be caught with his pants down. Ask for whatever you need and we'll see that you get it. Call Buckley here anytime you feel it's necessary. Just make sure you keep us posted."

The governor got up, shook Sam's hand, excused himself and left.

"He likes you," said Buckley. "Believe me, I know the governor and I'm telling you, he likes you, Captain."

"The man just met me," Sam protested.

"Yeah, well, think about it. Yesterday he has this conversation with Carlton Weimer, and he knows that I have a meeting today with the man in charge of the investigation. As I said, I know the governor and you can bet your life that he made damn sure that everything he needed to know about you was in front of him before ten o'clock this morning. Obviously, he liked what he read. Meeting you just sealed the deal. Believe me, Sam, you solve this thing and keep the governor from embarrassment, and you can name you own ticket."

Sam thanked the state's attorney and took his leave. There was work to do back in Essex. As soon as Sam began the trip south down route 9, he put in a call to Chief Taft. When the chief didn't answer, Sam called the front desk at the station house. The sergeant on duty informed Sam that Chief Taft had not come back from New Haven. He told the sergeant that he would be in New Haven for some time to run down a few new leads. Sam called the New Haven Police and they informed him that they were under the impression that the chief had left for Saybrook around four p.m. There was no reason for him to stay in New Haven any longer. The chief was a widower, so Sam was not surprised that there was no answer at his residence.

Sam knew that the chief always kept in touch with the precinct. He began to get concerned.

CHAPTER 5

Sam pulled up to the State Police barracks and checked in at the front desk. He immediately went to his office to see if there was any word on Chief Taft. Taft was still missing and now the authorities in Old Saybrook were starting to get worried. The chief had never done anything like this; he made it a practice to be in constant contact with the station house. Sam knew that this was not a good sign.

"Taft must have found out something down in New Haven and decided to act on it," Sam reasoned. His mind was racing to try to formulate a plan of action. No one saw the chief leave New Haven, so Sam had nowhere to begin. If the chief didn't turn up by the next morning, Sam would head down to talk to some of his friends at New Haven Police headquarters. He decided to go to the chief's house, something that no one had done yet. How the chief was missing all this time, and nobody thought to investigate his home was something Sam could not comprehend.

"We called over there a few times," the desk sergeant had informed him, "but got no answer. We just figured that he wasn't there." Sam shook his head in total disbelief.

"What if the chief were sick, or worse, had a heart attack?" he wondered. "How do those incompetents rationalize taking no action whatsoever?" he wanted to know. Sam's emotions were going from worry to anger, and then back to worry.

The chief lived alone in Westbrook, just south of Old Saybrook. Taft lived in a quiet area near the water. It took some time to locate the right road. There was only one other house on the street. Sam observed a family on the lawn of that home. It looked like the inhabitants were either packing or unpacking for a trip. He wanted to talk to them if there were no signs of life at the chief's house. Maybe they saw the chief.

Sam located the chief's house. There was no car in the carport. Slowly, he drove up the driveway and stopped. Sam exited his vehicle and took a good look around before heading to the front door. He rang the bell twice and waited a few minutes. There was no response. He walked over to one of the windows and looked in. Everything seemed to be in order, no signs of any wrongdoing. He cautiously made his way to the back door and froze. One of the small windows had been broken. For the first time in years, Sam drew his weapon. He pulled out his handkerchief and gently turned the doorknob so as not to disturb any fingerprints that might be on it. He walked a few steps across the back porch and saw the back door forced open. He eased the door open and entered. Sam moved slowly through the kitchen, all the while listening intently for any sounds in the house. All he heard was an eerie silence. He made his way from room to room, but no one was there. The kitchen was clean and the chief's bed neatly made. Sam found the door to the cellar and opened it. The light clicked on at his touch, and he descended the stairs. Once again, all was in order except for a metal filing cabinet in a far corner. Sam made sure that no one was in the cellar, and then went to investigate. He came across one drawer ransacked with its contents lying on the cellar floor. There was no way of knowing what was in the drawer or what someone was looking for, so Sam went back upstairs and left the house to try to catch the chief's neighbors.

He needn't have worried. The family had just come home from a camping trip, arriving only moments before Sam. Obviously, they were of no help. Whoever went through Taft's home had to be confident they wouldn't be interrupted. That only meant one thing as far as Sam was concerned. He thanked the people and headed off towards Old Saybrook as fast as possible. He used his siren and flashing lights to clear the way. In ten minutes, he roared up to the Old Saybrook police station and ran inside.

"Any word?" he demanded.

"Not a one, sir," was the officer's response.

"Show me the chief's office," Sam ordered.

Sam burst into the office, which was down the hall, tucked away from the main reception room and the jail cells. Just as he suspected, someone had tampered with the files and appeared to have taken some.

"Is there somebody on the desk at all times?" he asked the officer.

"Yes, sir," came the response.

"All twenty-four hours?" he asked.

"Well yes, sir, absolutely."

Sam thought for a second.

"Any other entrances to the building?" he asked.

"Uh, yeah," said the officer, "right there." The officer pointed to a door, a mere ten feet from the chief's office.

"Where does it lead?" Sam asked.

"The side of the building," offered the officer. "It's only a short walk to the back parking lot."

"Is it locked?" Sam wanted to know.

"Yes, sir, always."

Sam walked through the door and closed it behind him. Sure enough, he found the back entrance obscured from view. Next, he turned the doorknob and the door opened. Sam walked back inside.

"Really?" was all he said to the embarrassed and confused officer.

"I, I don't know how that could have happened," stammered the poor policeman.

"I'm shocked," Sam deadpanned, his eyes full of disgust while staring straight into those of the helpless desk officer.

"What price security?" Sam mocked.

The officer knew better than to say anything.

"Who's next in command?" asked Sam.

"I'm not really sure, but I guess that would be me," the officer said, probably wishing he had another answer.

Sam just stood there a minute and then told him to call the mayor immediately. Grudgingly, Sam was beginning to allow himself to accept the idea that Taft was not coming back. Whoever went through his office had probably made sure of that.

The mayor showed up in less than ten minutes, followed closely by some of the town council members. They gathered in the chief's office.

"The sergeant informs me that he might be in charge if the chief is not available. Is that true?" asked Sam to a room full of people who did not want to answer that question.

Finally, the mayor answered.

"I guess that's true, Sam. We've never had this happen before. You know this community; murders and police chiefs' disappearances just don't happen around here."

"Until now," said Sam.

"Yeah, until now," the mayor said reluctantly.

"Don't you people know that I have to file a report with the state's attorney's office? Just what am I supposed to tell them? Ethan Taft is one hell of a law enforcement officer. Sergeant what's his name is . . . . Sam paused, "a desk sergeant?" he finished. "For goodness sake, Mayor, how can you people be content with a one man police force?" Sam asked.

"What should we do, Sam?" asked the mayor.

Sam noticed that not one member of the town council had said a word.

"This would never happen in Essex," he told himself. "You couldn't keep the members of our town council quiet for even a minute."

"Right now, nothing," was Sam's answer. "But if Chief Taft doesn't show up soon, or if something has happened to him, you'd better hit the associated press wires and start advertising for a new chief, pronto. And Mayor, you have a five-town jurisdiction. You'd better get this police force of yours, if that's what you want to call it, better trained. For crying out loud, it appears that the chief's office was ransacked right under their noses," said Sam, in not too friendly a tone.

A collective groan rose up from the council members.

"How many men do you have on the force right now?" Sam asked.

"Eight, not counting the chief," said the mayor.

Sam was nearly speechless.

"There are only eight men to cover about four hundred square miles?" Sam asked.

"It's the funding, Sam," responded the mayor. "We just don't have the funds. And besides . . . ."

Sam cut him short. "Please don't say 'Nothing like this ever happens around here'."

Sam was having a difficult time masking his disdain for the local politicos.

"We live in one of the wealthiest parts of the state and these people can't come up with enough money to support an adequate police force," he thought to himself.

"Well, gentlemen, I'll put in a call to the attorney general and ask him how we should proceed. For now, I'd suggest you have the whole force on round the clock alert. We'd better find the chief, and fast. I'm going to bring in some of my men from over in Clinton. It's time we issued an all points bulletin on the chief. Say your prayers gentlemen, but it doesn't look good," Sam informed them.

Just then, Sam noticed there were two pages ripped from the chief's note pad. He also noticed the indentation of letters on the sheet facing him. He took a pencil and shaded over the indentations. The word "Manhattan" appeared.

"Does 'Manhattan' mean anything to anyone here?" Sam asked.

No one had a clue.

Sam was not surprised. He excused the group and then spoke to the desk sergeant. The sergeant in turn called the other officers to see if anyone knew anything. No one had any idea what Manhattan meant.

Dinner was a quiet affair at Aunt Clara's. It was obvious that Sam was deeply troubled, so everyone did their best to leave him to his thoughts. Wanda Loomis came to pick up the girls for a sleepover at her house with her girls. Thomas was thrilled to have some time to himself without the presence of his noisy sisters who constantly annoyed him with their unceasing chatter. It seemed to Thomas that the favorite activity of most females was talking. Thomas much preferred peaceful contemplation, something he experienced little of whenever the girls were around, and it seemed to Thomas that they were always around. Aunt Clara stayed with him while Martha and Sam took a walk up Main Street towards the park.

"Things aren't looking good for the chief, are they?" Martha asked as they walked.

Sam was finding words hard to come by. He really liked Ethan Taft; he sure respected him. He and the chief had known each other for fifteen years.

"We had a common bond, Ethan and I," Sam began. "We both lost our wives too early. Ethan knew his wife all his life. They went to grammar school and high school together. That's the way it is for most folks around here. You grow up and marry the person you think you're going to grow old with and then, well, things just don't work out the way you planned. Ethan's a loner. He doesn't have too many people in his life, just can't seem to fit them in, he doesn't know how to act. The man spends all his time reading; reads more books than you could ever imagine, reads everything. Folks say Ethan married the only woman he ever had a relationship with. Hell, those two knew each other eighteen years before Ethan asked her to marry him. When she died, Ethan closed the books on that part of his life. It just didn't seem possible to spend another eighteen years getting to know someone else. Besides, he probably never felt comfortable with another woman. I sure hope he's still around to give it another try though," said Sam.

Martha drew close to Sam and placed her arm around him.

"Let's go down by the water," she said.

They passed the gazebo and walked down to the water of the Middle Cove.

"Tell me about Aunt Clara," said Martha. "I find her fascinating. Why did she never marry? And what's with her and Injun Jim? That's a strange brew."

Sam had to laugh. "That takes in a whole lot of territory, but I'll try to answer as best I can. Talk is that Aunt Clara fell in love with a fisherman from Saybrook. I'm not really sure how they met, but I do know that my grandfather was furious with her for taking up with a man of little means and no breeding. He couldn't understand why she didn't choose someone from the local stock. Most of the men around here wouldn't stand a chance with a woman like Aunt Clara, as you probably can guess."

Martha totally agreed.

"Anyway, Aunt Clara really defied her father until my grandmother took suddenly ill. She had to choose between love and duty. Being the person she is, she chose duty. From that day on, she refused to speak to the fisherman. The man was brokenhearted. He went out to sea on a dangerously foggy day disregarding the warnings of his mates. He never returned. No one ever heard from him. There was never any sighting of him or his boat. When Aunt Clara heard the news, she went over to the church and prayed for a whole day. She was inconsolable. But the next day, she got up and got on with her life, a life of caring for my grandparents. They left almost everything to her when they passed on. My dad was successful in his own right. He was happy for her. They were very close. When my dad died, Aunt Clara adopted me, so to speak. I don't know what I'd do without her. As for Injun Jim, I guess you might say that she adopted him too. Men of the sea have a special place in Aunt Clara's heart. Injun Jim has nobody. He just showed up one day asking if he could do odd jobs to supplement his salary at the boatyard. He's intensely loyal to Aunt Clara for giving him a chance when no one else would. They're really something, the two of them, aren't they?"

Martha looked up at Sam and smiled. "That's a lovely story, Sam. Thank you for sharing it with me."

The two stood silently by the water and then Martha started to suppress a laugh. Sam looked down at her and asked, "What are you thinking about?"

"You almost kissed me here, I think," she said with a smile.

"Missed opportunities," said Sam, "one of a few, as I recall."

"But not lost," said Martha.

"I'm really glad to hear that," said Sam. "If there weren't all these folks here, I might just do something rash," he said.

"What a delightful thought," said Martha.

"Aunt Clara tells me you're going down to Yale tomorrow; how come?" Sam asked.

"Well first there's the matter of my hair. I have an appointment with a Mr. Phillip at Edwin Malley's. But mostly it's Peter Childers and his wife Elizabeth, my old friends from Columbia. They're both at Yale now and I thought as I'm so close, I'd love to go see them. Lizzy and I really raised hell at Cornell. Peter is a bit of a stiff but he's really a sweetie. Will you miss me?" she asked.

"How long will you be gone?" asked Sam.

"Overnight, but does it matter?"

"I just meant would you be gone long enough to miss?" teased Sam.

"Well, will you?"

"I miss you already," said Sam.

Martha buried herself in Sam's chest. She knew people took notice, but Sam was the first real man she had ever known. If someone were going to stop her, that someone would have to be Sam.

Sam pulled her closer.

The next morning, Sam put Martha on the 9:17 a.m. train headed for New Haven. He barely got settled into his cruiser when he got the word.

"Sorry to have to tell you this, sir, but Chief Taft's body just washed up on Goose Island. Some guys fishing over there found it about a half hour ago. It took them this long to get to a phone. We got people on the way. The Coast Guard is sending people," said the officer.

"Are they sure it's Ethan?" asked Sam.

"Well, all they can go by is the uniform and name plate. That's all we have to go on for now, sir. Shall we send a boat for you?"

"No, I'll get there myself," said Sam.

Sam called Aunt Clara and asked her to call Injun Jim. Sam pulled up to the dock at Wolf Harbor where Injun Jim was waiting. They sped off to Goose Island, southeast of Essex on the Connecticut River, just off the coast of Lyme.

Sam identified the body of his old friend. He was surprised to see that the chief had been shot twice in the chest with what appeared to be a small caliber weapon. As confusing as things were becoming, Sam got the strange feeling that a mystery was beginning to unravel. Now Sam had to have Ethan transported to Meriden and the police forensics lab.

"Ethan, Ethan," he said in a low, sad voice, "what did you uncover, old friend?"

Martha couldn't suppress her excitement. Lizzy Childers was her dearest college chum. Marty and Lizzy roomed together for three "gloriously irreverent years" at the upstate Halls of Ivy. Like all Ivy League schools, Cornell was a bastion of the understated, with just the proper tinge of snobbishness thrown in. Ivy leaguers were the best of the richest, and certainly, they represented the most respectable of the wealthy class and academia. Martha shared a laugh with herself as she fondly remembered how she and Lizzy spent years trying to figure out how two delinquents such as themselves gained acceptance. Both women placed in the top three percent of their class, but neither pledged a sorority, a circumstance that left the exalted sisterhood mystified and aghast.

Martha stepped onto the platform, looked left, and then right. It was a loud cry "Marty," followed by a shriek coming from a woman with long straight hair, dressed in 1935-college professor apparel that made Martha focus her attention on a woman charging down the platform in her direction. Elizabeth Childers came to an abrupt halt just inches from Martha and then threw her arms around her old friend and hugged with all her might. Martha hugged back, but not quite so strenuously. Elizabeth released her grip and stood back a few feet.

"Just look at you, you're absolutely gorgeous," she exclaimed. "The pictures on your book jackets don't do you a bit of justice. You know, Marty, you really should talk to your people about . . . ."

"Liz, Liz," interrupted Martha, "it's great to see you too. You look like . . . ." she groped.

"Those professors we made so much fun of back in school." Liz finished. "Oh, don't be shy, honey, little did I know back then that you had to look and dress like this to be accepted in the rarefied air of the Ivy League. Thanks to Peter, I sold out. He'll never be anything but a college professor, so here we are. But let me tell you, occasionally we steal away for a weekend at an inn upstate and then, boy, all hell breaks loose. I mean vamp underwear, skinny dipping in the lake under the moonlight . . . ."

Once again, Martha had to put a halt to Elizabeth's ramblings.

"It's slightly hot out here. Do you think we could go to your place so I can freshen up?" she asked.

"Oh, for goodness sakes, sure we can. It's just so good to see you, I couldn't help myself," said Liz.

The two women made their way arm and arm down the platform to the taxi station.

"139 Wooster Street," Elizabeth instructed the cabby.

It took only a few minutes riding through pleasant tree lined streets to reach the Wooster Street address in the heart of the Italian section of New Haven.

"We're only five minutes or so from the campus," said Liz. "No women living on campus at Yale, you know. That's quite alright with us though. Peter and I just love this neighborhood, and the food is the best in New Haven."

The women ascended the stairs to the Childers' four room second floor apartment. Martha walked in and found herself standing in the middle of the living room. She glanced around to observe bookcases filled to over-flowing, big comfortable furniture, a large central coffee table, plants everywhere and pictures hung tastefully on whitewashed walls; "early academia" Martha told herself.

Liz showed Martha the rest of the apartment, which matched the feel of the living room.

"A perfect example for 'Young College Professional Life'," Martha silently amused.

"Peter's an early riser so the bathroom is usually free after seven," said Liz. "Why don't you freshen up now and I'll make some tea. You still drink tea, don't you?" she asked.

"Absolutely," answered Martha.

"Oh Marty, it's just so good to see you; I've missed you so much," said Liz.

Four years had somehow come and gone since Liz and Martha spent a few highly enjoyable days in New York. As Martha stood there, she realized how much Liz meant to her. She couldn't believe that so much time had passed, but she was sure of one thing, it was she and not Liz who was the guilty party here.

"That goes double for me, my friend. Let's never allow so much time to pass between us again," she said, and deep inside, she really meant it.

Martha freshened up and joined Liz in the living room for tea and some girls catching up talk. After thirty minutes of delightful gossip, Liz instructed Martha that the two of them were going to meet Peter for lunch at Castaloni's Restaurant just down the street. Castaloni's had a back-yard patio where meals were served in the warm months. As Liz and Martha walked down Wooster Street, Liz exchanged pleasantries with some of the neighborhood locals. Martha noticed how completely at home Liz was. There was something serene in Liz's demeanor. Martha concluded that it seemed as though Liz had found the perfect life for herself. It was good to see her friend so happy. It struck her strange that Liz found such happiness in a life that was peaceful yet predictable and uneventful, as Martha saw it. Martha reasoned that her life up till now had been exciting, mildly chaotic and generally empty. No amount of money, fame, or prestige had even remotely given her what her dear friend appeared to have so comfortably acquired.

"Here we are," said Liz, leading Martha into an alleyway that led to the restaurant patio. Tucked nicely between the backyards of the neighboring homes, the restaurant was a throwback to home style dining from the old country, serving a Sicilian fare with lots of fresh produce and cheeses. The scene suggested an outside dining experience reminiscent of the Italian countryside. Castaloni's also baked their own bread. The smell coming from their basement bakery was heavenly.

No sooner had the ladies been led to their seats and settled in, Peter emerged from the alley. He made his way over to the table as Martha stood to great him.

"Wow" he said looking at Martha. "Geese, Marty, when did you get so glamorous?" he asked. "You'll cause a darn riot on campus for sure," he exclaimed.

Liz put her hands over her mouth. Peter was usually shy with most people until he got to know them, but Martha always seemed to loosen him up with ease. Peter always looked upon Martha as a sister to Liz. He and Liz considered her family. To the contrary, eight years of marriage and a host of holiday and periodic visits did little to thaw the relationship Peter had with Liz's family. Her people were old money while Peter's lineage was just old. No matter how many times Liz's family summoned Peter and Liz to their compound in Philadelphia, the climate was pure winter. They never got over Liz's decision to marry out of her class.

Peter threw his arms around Martha and lifted her off the ground.

"Peter, for goodness sakes," scolded Liz. "Put her down, you'll cause a scandal."

"Oh, come on now," retorted Peter, "how many people in our circle can claim to hobnob with the rich and famous?"

"And beautiful," added Liz.

"Yes, beautiful," Peter agreed.

"How on earth did that happen?" kidded Peter, feigning mock astonishment.

"Alright, alright, that will be quite enough, Mr. Childers," scolded Martha. I can see where this is going and I'll have none of it."

Everyone shared a laugh and then Peter reached across the table and took Martha's hand. "We've both missed you so much. Liz and I speak of you all the time. You are never out of our minds."

Peter's words caught Martha by surprise. Before she could react, a tear started to stream down her face. She wiped it away self-consciously.

"Good Lord, Peter," she said, "you're making me cry."

Peter looked over to his wife who was gently wiping away her own tear.

Peter ordered lunch, family style, light but deliciously satisfying. A mixture of pasta, salad and finale of fruit followed a beginning of fresh baked bread and generous portions of moist table cheese. After an hour or so, Peter looked at his watch and exclaimed! "It's almost one o'clock and our ride will be arriving out front." Peter paid the bill, thanked the waiter, and led the ladies to the street. Almost on cue, a large four-door Buick sedan pulled up to the curb. Peter opened the rear door to allow Martha and Liz to climb in and then got in the front passenger seat.

"This is Phillip," Peter announced. "Phillip works for the university. It is Phillip's job to escort our most prestigious visitors. Phillip, meet Martha Frost."

Phillip looked into his rearview mirror and when his eyes met Martha's he gave a wave.

"It is a pleasure to serve you, Miss Frost. I hope you will enjoy your visit to Yale," said the driver.

Martha was slightly embarrassed.

"Thank you, Phillip," said Martha. "I wonder, could you oblige me by naming some of the other visitors you have escorted recently?" Phillip took a few seconds to respond.

"Well, let me see," said Phillip. "There was the Duke of Wales, Rear Admiral Nimetz, various military brass, Greta Garbo, Betty Davis, Albert Einstein, Samuel Goldwin, Sr., Clarke Gable, members of the Mellon family and, oh yes, the young Miss Shirley Temple. And might I be so bold, Miss Temple is growing into quite a young lady."

Martha tapped Peter on the shoulder. "Nice going, Peter," she said sarcastically, "how good of you to include me in such an esteemed group of people."

"Would that be enough, Miss Frost?" Peter inquired.

"Oh yes, that will be just fine," answered an exasperated Martha.

Liz took hold of Martha's arm and patted it gently. "It's just that Peter thinks you are such a big deal. He's so proud of you, Marty," Liz informed her friend.

Martha turned to look at Liz. "Yes, well that and the anticipation of coming events is beginning to scare me," she told her friend.

"I promise, Peter will be on his best behavior," Liz assured her.

"Ah, we're here," announced Peter.

The three exited the large Buick and Peter leaned to give Phillip instructions.

"No tour of Yale should ever begin without first visiting the old campus," Peter announced.

With that, he positioned himself between both ladies, took each by an arm and walked them up Chapel Street towards College, lecturing all the way.

Sam was a veteran police officer, but staring down at the bare lifeless body of his friend Ethan Taft was hard to take. No autopsies took place until a family member or friend identified the body. Sam knew that Ethan had no family, so he was it.

"You two knew each other pretty well, didn't you?" asked the chief medical examiner, Howard Grimes.

"Yes," came Sam's barely audible response.

Howard placed a hand on Sam's shoulder, a sign of compassion.

"It's hard to lose a friend this way," said Howard.

Sam did not respond, but stepped away from the table to a place at the far end of the room and allowed his body to collapse against the wall.

"It's going to take some time before I'll have anything for you, but I've got some info you might be interested in on that other case," said Grimes.

Sam came to attention at Grimes' comment. "Really, like what?" he asked.

"You think these two crimes might be linked together don't you?" he said, not expecting an answer. "Well, I've got news and I've got some thoughts. First off, I know that Findley thinks that this case is going to be his ticket to the big time. I've seen him in action and believe me, it isn't pretty. Weimer's people, on the other hand, are relentless. They call all hours of the day asking the craziest questions, but my feeling is that they'll attack Fine's case from every imaginable angle and some unimaginable. But here's the kicker, Sam; both sides are going to address the competency of this facility. I'm sure of that. Weimer's people will argue that we are a new kid on the block and they'll be dragging up all kinds of evidence of forensic incompetence from every case they can; and believe me, Sam, there's a lot of incompetence in this field. Most states and municipalities don't even use people trained or experienced in forensic sciences. Hell, medical schools won't even consider adding it to the curriculum."

"You're painting a wonderful picture for me, Howard," said Sam.

"Ah, but don't despair, my friend. There's good news here. First, let me assure you that I am very experienced in forensic science, especially where fingerprints are concerned. We use an age-old method called the Vecutich system that dates back to the late 19th century. It requires sixteen matching points to confirm identity. The State of Connecticut only requires eleven points, but I got sixteen off that pipe they brought in."

Sam's spirits plummeted. This was not good news for the Ruckers.

"Oh boy," Sam moaned.

Grimes was not through. "Let's not get ahead of ourselves here, Captain. Remember every crime depends on three things."

"Motive, means and opportunity," said Sam.

"Exactly," sprang Grimes. "We've got the pipe, we've got the fingerprints and we've established that the blood on the pipe was human and looks as though it is the same type as the victim's," said the examiner.

"And this is the good news you alluded to?" asked Sam.

Grimes hesitated for a moment for a dramatic pause. He loved these rare moments when he imparted something obvious but not yet recognized by the police. Oh, the medical examiner's life was a lonely one.

"A little too close to this case, don't you think, Captain?" queried the examiner, knowing the answer. "Think, Sam, what's missing?"

"A case?" offered Sam.

Grimes had to laugh at that one. He was one of the few people who appreciated Sam's dry sense of humor.

"Let's look at what we've got. First, a wooden object hit the victim repeatedly. Tests from the skull fragments are consistent with the wood used to make oars. Next, indentations of the skull suggest a heavy metal pipe finished the job, sometime later. Blood vessels under the skin confirmed that he was not dead from the first attack. The activity of the blood suggests that the body had already begun the healing process. The pipe blows definitely came later. But something is missing, Sam. Come on, man, think," prodded Grimes.

Sam took a minute and then it all came clear. "The mess," he exclaimed. "There should have been blood all over Rucker and his clothes. We found no blood anywhere. And from what I hear, Rucker had been wearing the same clothes for days. Witnesses have confirmed that. There was no blood on his hands, on his clothes, in his room, his car, no blood anywhere. That's just not possible."

"I'm sure Weimer's people will come to the same conclusions. I have a feeling that Findley is in for a rough ride. He had better not get his hopes up too high on this one. Weimer will clobber any attempts to prove that the Rucker boy killed Weiss. Beyond reasonable doubt and all that," said Grimes.

"Howard, I could hug you," said Sam.

"Control yourself," was Grimes' dry advice to him. "Now go get a cup of coffee and let me get to work. Give me an hour and I'll have something for you."

True to his word, one hour later, Grimes sought Sam out and gave him his report.

"This is a preliminary, you understand, but there's more here than what we see on the surface; there always is, you know. Well, anyway, here's what we got. It appears that the chief was shot at close range initially and then once again as he staggered back, by a pistol of German origin. The two bullets we removed were from a .45 caliber Luger eight clip."

Sam received the news well. He finally had something to go on beyond fingering a drunken Robert Rucker. Sam had no idea where this was going, but he was sure that Robert was just a pawn. Something else crossed his mind. Whoever framed Robert knew him. That threw a completely new light on the case. If someone local was involved, then Essex wasn't as safe for the townspeople as Sam had originally believed. Sam didn't want to accept that someone he knew was a killer, but the idea that one of the locals might be an accomplice was starting to become a real possibility.

The mud was getting clearer, but it was still mud.

"It appears as though Ethan tried to get the gun away from his killer. But the gun went off. There are powder burns on the clothes. The water around here is not warm enough to destroy the evidence. Actually, it is just cold enough to preserve it. But the burns only appear on one of the wounds. It seems likely that Ethan fell back and the shooter shot him again at point blank range. I think Ethan knew the man, Sam. He was too good a cop to have someone unknown surprise him. I believe Ethan felt secure before he was shot, probably taken by complete surprise. Of course, the shooting could have happened the other way around. The killer shot him at close range and then moved in for another. No way to know right now, but we'll examine him further and let you know for sure."

Sam thanked Grimes for all the details as well for sharing his thoughts. All Sam had to do now was to wait for confirmation.

"One thing," cautioned Grimes. "If it did happen in reverse order, we've got one dangerous person in our midst. A shooting like that is real cold-blooded. Someone capable of that could be capable of anything," warned Grimes.

"And I was just feeling better about things," said Sam.

"Enjoy," said Grimes as he turned to go back to his work.

As night came, Sam lowered his exhausted body onto his bed. Tomorrow he'd go to New Haven to talk to the guys who spoke with Ethan. Something they told Ethan pointed him in the direction of his death. Forty miles away, Martha too was lying on Liz's large living room couch after a long day of sightseeing with her friends. As sleep came to both of them, they shared a common thought; they both really missed each other.

CHAPTER 6

On January 10, 1916, Martha Emerson Frost made a rather loud and painful entry into the world. Her mother Eleanor had endured thirty-three hours of merciless labor. Eleanor was sure this was her punishment for the one unguarded passionate night she had with her stiff as a board husband, Nigel Frost. In later years, she quipped to her friends that no one had a more suitable last name than her husband did. The blessed event did not thrill either parent. They realized that neither was exactly what one might describe as parent material. Many of their well-healed friends had nannies to make family life more bearable. The Frosts were of the literati class, highly educated, much in demand dinner guests, respected and tenured, poor as church mice. Their strength was their highly developed intellect. They were soon to add to their vast storage of knowledge the unpleasant realization that they were no match for the only child they would ever parent.

Long before she could walk or talk, Martha's instincts told her that she could easily manipulate these overmatched, helpless in her presence individuals who bore the title "parents." On the evening of Martha's first day away at Cornell, her parents threw the party of the year in Kingston, Vermont.

Martha came home for Thanksgiving that first year, a practice she seldom repeated over the next five years. Once she hooked up with Lizzy Clairmont, a product of Philadelphia wealth and social standing, she found little reason to ever venture back to the hills of Vermont. The Clairmonts adopted Lizzy's remarkable young friend and introduced Martha to the world of wealth, power and high society. The simple truth was, for all their worth, the Clairmonts were not a warm and loving couple, but welcomed Martha as one of their own. The senior Clairmont encouraged Martha to write her first novel.

Martha's father envisioned himself a writer. Martha remembered well the bitter disappointment he suffered with each rejection of his proposed works. Nigel Frost's coldness leaped from the pages of his novels and the truth was that the public was not in the mood for his tragedies and morose renderings. He wrote well, he just lacked a heart.

It was during her postgraduate studies that Martha told Lizzy about this crazy idea she had for a story. Lizzy was very enthusiastic and encouraging, so Martha started to write in her spare time. When Lizzy read the completed manuscript, she begged her closest friend to let the senior Clairmont look at it. When Lizzy's father could not put the thing down until he finished reading it, Lizzy was convinced that Martha was really on to something.

When Columbia in New York City, the publishing capital of the world, offered Martha a position, Lizzy sprang into action. She got her father to use his contacts to get the manuscript to someone of importance at Harcourt Press. Enter Ellen Gold and the dawning of a highly successful writing career of one twenty-two year old associate professor at Columbia.

The shock of Martha's success left her parents stunned with disbelief. Nigel Frost's utter failure as a writer, although he did have articles published in academic journals, and his daughter's meteoric success helped cement a lasting chill that neither side was willing to ease. Although Martha's life in New York was nowhere near as successful as her writing career, she never felt the compulsion to run home to mommy and daddy. Conversely, the Clairmonts supplied needed solace when things got tough. And then, the long absences. Martha could not explain it, it just happened. She pledged anew to right that wrong.

It was just past one p.m. when Sam pulled into the visitor's parking lot of police headquarters for the city of New Haven. Sergeant Matt Donofrio was waiting for him in the main vestibule.

"Leave it to the war to give you valley guys a reason to not take a beating this year," the sergeant announced.

"Oh, yeah," Sam shot back, "word has it that you guys were ready to bring in ringers from the Bronx; couldn't stand getting your heads handed to you by a bunch of yokels, and superior yokels at that."

The two men laughed, shook hands, and embraced. The annual summer baseball games between the various police and fire departments from New Haven to New London had created a chain of camaraderie up and down the Connecticut coast. The rivalries had become intense, but the friendships created had succeeded in breaking down many barriers while greatly aiding in the setting up of a network of communication and cooperation that proved beneficial to all. Sergeant Donofrio led Sam to his office and then ordered coffee for both from his aide.

"Make a fresh pot, paisano," he exploded. "None of your stale motor oil for our honored guest," said the sergeant, while making a good-natured gesture towards Sam.

"Sorry to hear about Ethan," said Donofrio. "I really liked that guy. He was a good cop. Those people in Saybrook will have a tough time replacing him." Sam nodded in agreement. "I called the two detectives he met with. They should be here any minute now. They told me they'd be glad to help in any way they can. I know these guys, Sam. They'll be straight with you."

Sam thanked the sergeant and as the two men waited for their coffee; they got into a heated discussion about team rosters and the strengths and weaknesses of their respective ball teams. The war had taken some good players from both sides. Both men agreed that the only important issue here was that all those guys come home safe and sound.

Sam had just downed his second cup of fresh brewed coffee when a knock at the door signaled the arrival of Detectives Roland and Lacey. Both detectives were from the homicide division. Sam was most interested to learn how two homicide detectives from New Haven had been of service to Chief Taft.

"Chief Taft asked us a lot, questions about foreigners being involved in homicides committed in New Haven over the last year or so. He seemed to be placing a heavy emphasis on people of German descent or possibly political sympathizers to the German cause," said Lacey.

"Yeah," piped in Roland, "he kept asking questions about visitors at Yale, foreign visitors. He seemed like he knew what he was looking for; he just needed us to fill in the blanks. We showed him all our files for the last eighteen months. The man read every one. It took him a few hours."

Lacey jumped in "We can't tell you if he got what he wanted, but he thanked us and said he was going back to Saybrook. That was about four p.m. He took off in the wrong direction, but we just assumed he found his way. New Haven's street layout is a nightmare if you don't know your way. Next thing we hear, the chief is dead. We figured he must have found something, but we couldn't tell you what it was. Roland and I made a quick review of those cases but came up empty. You're welcome to go through them if you like. Maybe something there will be familiar to you."

Sam took them up on their offer. He spent the next few hours going over all the cases Ethan had investigated. Sam wasn't sure what to look for, so he tried to get a read on each one so that he might come back to them later if necessary. Most of the domestic violence murders ruled themselves out. The same applied to deaths because of failed robbery attempts. That left forty-one cases that Sam tried to familiarize himself with; down the line, one might just prove helpful.

Sam checked back with Donofrio and made his goodbyes. It was close to five thirty and he had promised to meet Martha and her friends at Castaloni's Patio. Traffic at this hour of the day made the short trip to Wooster Street longer than normal. Sam parked illegally, but knew that the local cops would honor the State Police emblem on his license plates. The large trees in the neighborhood yards provided a welcome shade from the sun and the lights strung around the restaurant provided a lovely complement to the atmosphere.

"Oh my, Marty," said Liz as Sam walked across to join them.

"Hush," Martha scolded her friend.

Liz just gave her a "you never told me he was gorgeous," look.

Martha introduced Sam to her friends. A breaking the ice round of before dinner drinks turned into a one hour getting to know you event. Martha was astonished at the way her friends took to Sam. Liz was a regular chatterbox while Peter usually required some prodding. Within minutes, all were talking and laughing without reservation. Martha had quite forgotten that Sam had grown up a child of privilege. He had spent his high school years at Avon, one of the most exclusive prep schools in the country. The birth of Mary prompted his leaving Boston College after his second year. Not wanting to subject his family to the nomadic conditions of a military career, he opted to join the State Police. It took only three years for Sam to reach lieutenant rank. By the time Thomas came along he was being considered for captain. His rise was meteoric, but not surprising, as he always ranked near the top of his class in school.

"I see you've had your hair done," observed Sam.

"Do you like it?" Martha asked.

"What do you think?" asked Sam as he smiled and looked directly into her eyes.

Everyone at the table knew the answer to that.

Martha settled back thoroughly enjoying Sam and the Childers going on like old friends. Peter later confided to Liz how impressed he was with Sam. "How enjoyable," he declared, "and quite surprising to be with a policeman, of all people, with such breeding and intelligence."

Such was Peter's snobbishness. Sam, to his credit, recognized it early on and just played along. Martha made note of it. It pleased her a lot.

Dinner finally came. The food never interfered with the animated chatter of the group. It was now eight-thirty, time for Martha and Sam to be heading back to Wolf Harbor. Peter brought Martha's belongings down for her and he, Liz, and Martha embraced. After tearful goodbyes, Sam drove across town to catch Route 1, the Boston Post Road, taking them back to Essex.

It was quite dark by now, but it was a lovely star filled summer night. Route 1 hugged the coastline connecting many of the quaint seaside New England towns between New Haven and Essex. Sam was content just to be taking Martha back to the Tyler compound, but Martha was bursting to share the events of the past two days.

Yale was alive with military activity. Hundreds of Navy reserves and R.O.T.C. members of the student body did calisthenics on the green of the old campus. Early evidence of the military was everywhere. Every branch of the armed forces seemed to be present. Yale was quite proud of its history in times of war. It openly embraced the military presence. Peter and Liz had squired Martha everywhere including the campus of Yale's sister school, Albertus Magnus. The Gothic architecture of the great university was physically imposing, yet pleasing to the eyes. Everything about Yale sent a message that it took itself seriously. Still, there was a peaceful serenity about the place in spite of all the activity.

Peter had taken the girls over to the science building to introduce them to two visiting scientists, Charles Beekman and Nigel Forest. Beekman and Forest were at Yale to confer on a very hush hush project. They came to substantiate certain atomic equations that were vital to the war effort. Martha informed Sam that Peter had let the words "Manhattan Project" slip out after one drink too many at a local pub.

Martha's revelation quickened Sam's pulse. "Manhattan Project," he repeated. "I found that word 'Manhattan' on Chief Taft's office note pad," he informed Martha. "What on earth made a secret science project important to Ethan? It's obvious that the murders in Essex are somehow connected to this Manhattan Project. Weiss must have been on his way to meet those two scientists. I knew Ethan was one hell of a policeman, but how on earth did he make the connections so fast?" he asked.

"What makes you so sure he did make those connections?" Martha wanted to know.

"His death," said Sam, with sobering finality.

Martha paused for a moment absorbing the impact of Sam's answer. She then proceeded to tell him the further details of her campus visit. Everywhere she went there were deep philosophical discussions going on about the war and the condition of the world economy. It was quite startling to Martha to hear so many diverse opinions openly discussed. It was strange indeed to witness such conflicting positions taking place, existing in the same space without incident. Young men were preparing themselves to go to war while others were questioning just how the world got to such a place that fomented that war. Martha expressed concern that a new liberalism was emerging in the same environment where patriotism and support for the war abided.

Sam was trying to pay attention to Martha, but the realization that Ethan Taft was aware of the Manhattan Project and had somehow made a connection between it and the homicide at Wolf Harbor was posing a challenge.

"There's something else," said Martha, and then she was silent.

The silence caught Sam's attention.

"There's more?" asked Sam.

"Yes, said Martha, "and I must tell you it's quite disturbing."

"How so?" Sam inquired.

"Have you ever heard of the Skull and Bones Society?" Martha asked.

"Actually, I have," said Sam. "I remember overhearing a conversation at one of Arlen Templeton's parties. Two of his guests were having a heated discussion about it, but stopped talking when they realized I could hear what they were saying. I think they knew I was a law officer. I guess it's some sort of fraternity or club at Yale."

"Oh, it's more than a club Sam, much more than a club," said Martha. "The Skull and Bones have been around Yale and only Yale for over one hundred years. It is a most secret organization that seems to be open only to the most wealthy and select. Once in, you can never get out, or so that's what they say. They meet in a secret building called the 'tombs' and no one seems to know what goes on inside. Although there are many theories, believe me. Peter thought it great fun to show me where it is. God, Sam, the place is real spooky. Anyway, as a matter of pride, I guess Liz told me that if Peter had gone to Yale they would have chosen him. So many of the students idolize him, he's such a gifted thinker and debater; aptitudes not lost on the Skulls. Many students consider it an honor being invited to their apartment and be counted among Peter's inner circle. Liz just thinks it's great fun to have these young people express such lofty postulations, and of course, sing the praises of her husband. But Sam, I'm telling you these Skull people are frightening. First of all this society got its start in 1837 as the American chapter of a German order known as the Brotherhood of Death or simply chapter 322. I have no idea what the numbers represent. Neither does Peter. Anyway, one of its founders was the father of President Taft. Listed among the ranks are many of the families of the great banks and money institutions of our country. There are hints that these people funded Hitler and are behind the coming United Nations. I'm starting to think that your friend may have wandered into something of a far greater magnitude than he could ever have imagined."

Sam realized that they had reached the intersection of Route 153. They had been traveling for almost an hour and Martha had filled that space with volumes of information. Sam was astounded.

"You learned all of that in less than two days?" he asked.

"Why yes, yes I did, now that you mention it," said Martha in a most pleased tone of voice accompanied by a proud facial expression.

Sam let some space go by as they approached Essex.

"Your powers of observation are remarkable. No wonder you're such a good writer. You don't miss much, do you, Miss Frost?" asked Sam.

Martha did not answer, choosing to enjoy the favor of Sam's compliments.

Sam pulled the cruiser into his driveway. He and Martha walked around back and into the kitchen where Injun Jim was holding down the fort.

"The kids wanted to wait up to see you two, but they didn't make it. Thomas fell asleep around nine. The girls were out before that. Aunt Clara just went home. Guess I'll be going, too."

Sam thanked Injun Jim and went to check on the children. He came back moments later and then escorted Martha across the great lawn.

"Did you enjoy your visit?" Sam asked Martha.

"I know that you're thinking I spent all my time snooping around, but that's not true. Peter, Liz, and I had a great time. I didn't get much sleep though. Peter has so much energy. He dragged me everywhere. I just love the two of them. They really seemed to like you. Did you like my friends, Sam?" Martha asked.

"Yes," said Sam with a broad smile. "I think they're great. You must have had a lot of good times up at Cornell."

"Infamous is more like it," said Martha with a laugh.

Sam loved her laugh. When she did, her eyes sparkled and there was no trace of self-consciousness in her. Now they were on Aunt Clara's porch and Sam was standing there looking at Martha. Neither said anything. Finally, Sam reached for her and drew her closer. His lips found hers and Martha totally surrendered herself into Sam's strong arms. They kissed a long kiss and then released. Martha tried to say something, but Sam's mouth stopped her as once again she allowed herself to be overwhelmed in Sam's embrace. The second kiss was even longer than the first, overflowing in passion. Once again, Sam released her. This time she had no desire to speak.

"I've got to get back," he heard himself say. Leaving Martha was the last thing he wanted to do, but they weren't a couple of fifteen year olds and Aunt Clara would probably take a dim view of two grown adults "making out" on her back porch.

Sam started to pull back but Martha stopped him. She put her arms around him and placed her head into his chest. Finally, she released Sam, opened the screen door, and disappeared into Aunt Clara's kitchen.

Sam walked across the lawn with a head filled with a million thoughts. All that Martha had revealed had his mind racing. Then there was the matter of their embrace. Sam had to admit it, kissing Martha just made things even more confusing. It was foolhardy to think that a woman like Martha Frost would give up her life for one with a policeman from the sticks. How in hell was he going to handle her leaving?

Martha made her way to her quarters and started to undress. She had taken off her blouse and found herself just sitting on the bed. She had to admit to herself that she was confused. She also had to admit that she had never experienced a kiss like Sam's. His arms seemed like the safest place on earth. As if controlled by some outside force, Martha found herself standing up, putting her blouse back on, and heading down the back stairs.

Sam checked on the children once again. All three were peacefully slumbering. How Sam wished he could be that age again, without the cares of the world closing in all around him. He poured a glass of ice water from the refrigerator and went back outside to sit on the porch and enjoy the moonlight dancing off the waves of Wolf Harbor.

Sam looked in the direction of Aunt Clara's, having heard a sound coming from that direction. He looked up to see Martha coming towards him.

"Hi," he said, "anything wrong? Did you forget something?"

"Yes," said Martha, "I did."

With that, she sat in Sam's lap and crushed her mouth to his. Martha's passion surprised him. For a moment, he found himself completely overcome.

"I have no idea how this is going to work, but I just can't get enough of you, Samuel Tyler," said Martha as she caressed his face and once again kissed him full on the lips.

"That goes double for me, Martha Frost," countered Sam as he plunged his hands deeply into her thick mane and pulled her to him. Once again, they were speechless but the pounding of their hearts against each other's chest eliminated any need for words to justify their longings. This was the best night yet.

CHAPTER 7

Sam got up early the next morning. He had a lot on his mind. The events of the previous evening were weighing heavily on him, not making his life any simpler. He had to admit that the whole episode with Martha made him feel like a teenager once again. Sam really liked that feeling, but he had to be rational. He had to consider the effect on the children. A sobering thought interrupted Sam's verbal meanderings. What effect? Was he getting ahead of himself? The only thing settled last night was that he and Martha were going to find it difficult to keep their hands off one another. Sam had not kissed anyone nor been kissed by anyone like that since Sally. And no one, absolutely no one, had ever acted as boldly as Martha had; not with him anyway. But nothing had been resolved. In reality, things just got even more complicated.

Thomas and the girls came bounding down the stairs and into the kitchen. Sam looked up at the clock. "I believe Aunt Clara is waiting breakfast on you three," said Sam.

"Aunt Clara is making blueberry pancakes for us before we go," announced Lillith.

"Yeah, and I'm going to eat a whole stack," declared Thomas.

"You know, Thomas," said Mary, "gluttony is not really an admirable trait. I'm sure the starving children of this world will be just thrilled to hear how much food you are able to consume."

"Oh brother," Thomas responded, "here she goes again, Miss Right and Wrong."

Sam looked over to Lillith who just rolled her eyes.

"Come on, give me a hug and then scoot," bade Sam.

He hugged all three and sent them on their way over to Aunt Clara's. Watching them run across the lawn, the ringing telephone interrupted him. It was Arlen Templeton inviting him to join him over at the factory in Deep River. Arlen wanted Sam to witness a demonstration of one of the new gliders. The appointed time was eleven o'clock this morning. Sam had plenty of time.

Martha came downstairs just as the children were finishing their breakfast. She hugged the children and poured herself a cup of coffee.

"I called Sam," she said to Aunt Clara, "but there was no answer. Has he gone to work already?"

"I suspect he'd be at the cemetery up on North Main. He usually goes there to think. I'll have Injun Jim drive you over there if you like," offered Aunt Clara.

"That's okay," said Martha. "A walk is just what I need. If I don't start getting some exercise, I'm going to begin to resemble some of those cows I saw up by Deep River. I never knew I could eat so much food. It must be the air up here."

"I'm taking the children up river to the children's theater in East Haddam for a matinee puppet show. It's part of their summer series. We should be back around three this afternoon. Make yourself at home while we're gone," said Aunt Clara.

Martha said her good-byes and went out the back door towards Main Street. She walked up Main to the intersection of North Main and then on to the cemetery to try to meet up with Sam.

It took twenty minutes for Martha to reach the cemetery gates. She looked around, but did not see Sam. She started down the main pathway. She had only taken a few steps before she saw him walking towards her from down by the river. When Sam saw her, he waved and smiled. Martha was encouraged.

"Hi," he said when he reached the place where Martha was standing.

"I didn't want to come any closer and intrude," she said. "This is where your wife is, isn't it?" She asked.

Sam smiled. "Yes, it is," he said. "I like to come here to think. It's extremely peaceful. All my family and old friends are buried here. It's sort of a comfort to be here with them, you know."

Martha nodded, but did not speak.

"Come on, let's get a coffee at Nate's," said Sam.

They started to walk back towards Main Street when Martha gently took hold of Sam's arm and stopped.

"Can we talk?" she asked.

"Sure," said Sam. "What do you want to talk about?"

Martha half laughed. "Last night, today, tomorrow . . . us!" she said.

Sam hesitated then let out a deep breath.

"That's a whole lot of territory, isn't it?" he asked.

"Let's start with us," said Martha.

"So much for subtlety," said Sam.

Martha didn't hesitate. "I think I'm about to make a fool of myself, but here goes," Martha began. "I think I'm falling in love with you, but please hear me out. I'm not exactly lily white, and I'm not your girl next door. I don't know if I could ever measure up to Sally with you or the children or with anyone else for that matter. But I'm a one-man woman. I'm all the way or not at all." Martha paused for a moment. "Let me finish, please," she said before Sam could speak. "I've never felt this way before. I've never acted this way before. Oh, I've had relationships, for lack of a better word. And I've been linked in the tabloids with a few high profile gentlemen of New York Society, but that was not like this. I didn't sleep last night. No man has ever been able to do that to me. I can't stop thinking about you; no matter how hard I try, and believe me I try. I'm fast lane and you're country lane, and I must tell you, I'm really learning to cherish the country lane. Your children are simply wonderful. I feel so alive when I'm around them. Back in New York, I simply exist. And as for Aunt Clara, I'm speechless. But I want you to know that even if you don't or can't feel the same towards me, it has been worth it. I honestly never thought I'd ever experience love. My life in Manhattan is so shallow, so pretentious. Essex, Wolf Harbor, this is real. What I'm feeling is real, and I thank you for giving this to me. I'm falling in love with you, Samuel Tyler, and it is the best feeling I've ever experienced. Now I know what all the great love stories are about. To be honest with you, I thought they were the workings of the imaginations of some truly gifted writers. Now I know that it exists. You've shown me that in such a short time that it's quite shocking, but now that I've seen it, I know that it's real."

Sam looked down at Martha. He looked deeply into her eyes and knew what he had to say. "I've loved only one woman in my life, until now. I just never thought it would happen twice because I always felt so blessed. Now you come here and I'm feeling like it really can happen again. I have to admit that you're a better person than I am."

"What do you mean by that?" asked Martha.

"I couldn't be as magnanimous as you if you didn't feel the same," said Sam.

"And now that you know that I do?" asked Martha.

"I couldn't be happier. I love you, Martha Frost, but I'm also afraid of losing you, just when I've found you. What's to keep you here?'

"You, silly, and the children and Aunt Clara and haven't you heard a word I've said?" she demanded.

Sam did not answer with words. Instead, he gathered Martha in his arms and kissed her, right there on North Main Street with cars passing in either direction. Some teenager driving by yelled out to them. They both laughed but did not release each other.

"Let's go back to the house before we get arrested for unacceptable public behavior?" asked Martha.

"Just let them try," said Sam as he took her hand and led her towards Pratt Street and home.

Sam pulled into the Templeton driveway. Arlen was standing outside under the portico, waiting. He motioned for Sam to stop. Arlen walked over to the passenger side and got into Sam's car.

"Thanks for being so prompt," he said.

"Is William off today?" Sam inquired about the Templeton chauffer.

"I thought it would be nice for a change to not have to travel in that damn stuffy limo," Arlen said. "Besides, this is a police car. We can speed and no one can stop us," said Arlen with great pleasure.

Sam smiled and directed his vehicle north on North Main towards Deep River and the Pratt Reed and Company factory. The two men made small talk during the short ride.

"There are some high level brasses here from the Army," Arlen informed him. "The government has sunk a lot of money into this project. They want to see if it's been worth their investment."

"And has it?" asked Sam.

"Let's see for ourselves," said Arlen as he directed Sam to a secluded airstrip near the plant. The Army Corps of Engineers had installed it for easy access by the military.

Arlen jumped out of Sam's vehicle and made his way straight to a gathering of officers at the north end of the strip.

"Gentlemen, good to see you," said the affable Arlen.

The officers greeted him warmly, but with an air of reservation. Everyone was anxious to view the proceedings.

Sam parked his car and joined them. Arlen introduced him all around.

"We're starting a little early, sir," announced a lieutenant. "There's threat of a fog coming in so it is imperative that we begin immediately."

He no sooner had made his statement, than the roar from a huge four-engine cargo plane caught everyone's attention. The large plane was coming straight at the group. With a smaller box-like plane in tow, the cargo carrier started to lift off just a few hundred feet from the group. Soon it was directly overhead with a three hundred foot towline attached to a small wooden glider. It wasn't long before both were out of sight

"In a few minutes they'll work around to the south again and about two or three miles away the carrier will disconnect leaving the glider to operate on its own," Arlen told Sam.

Arlen then led the whole entourage to an area halfway down the landing strip. It wasn't long before the larger plane appeared and made a landing. After a few moments, the glider became visible over the tops of the trees at the south end of the field. The glider began a graceful descent and landed flawlessly, coming to a safe stop no more than one hundred feet from the group. The pilot got out, but before the military observers could applaud, they had a surprise, engineered by Arlen. Seven soldiers climbed out of the glider, disassembled the craft into a modular strike base, and then came to attention. The brass was impressed. Distributed out all around were laughs, handshakes, and slaps on the back. Sam stood back in amazement. Arlen Templeton owned the day. No wonder this man of simple beginnings enjoyed such an exalted status with the elite. There was more than a small touch of P.T. Barnum in Mr. Templeton. Arlen looked over at Sam and gave him a wink. Sam really enjoyed watching Arlen basking in his own glory.

Sam waited patiently until Arlen concluded his business and sent the military on their way. Arlen joined him and the two walked to Sam's car, and then made the short ride back to the Templeton home. Sam told Arlen how impressed he was by the demonstration.

"Our gliders will not be of much use on a major scale, but they could be of invaluable assistance for covert operations or small scale projects. Every edge we have makes our position that much stronger. Those Germans are a tough, smart bunch. They won't go down easily. Hitler has their heads filled with all kinds of nonsense. We have to chip away at their superman mentality. I believe it's already happening."

It was obvious that Arlen had a special place in his heart for Sam. They were always very comfortable in each other's company. As Sam pulled into the Templeton driveway, he decided to see if Arlen could shed some light on this secret group down at Yale. When he asked Arlen about the Skull and Bones, he noticed a definite change in attitude.

"What's your involvement with these people?" he asked Sam.

"None that I know of, but we've got so little to go on that I figured why not see what they're all about. Besides, I'm becoming increasingly convinced that Yale somehow figures heavily into this thing."

"Tread slowly and softly with the Skulls," cautioned Arlen. "These people are very powerful and can be very dangerous when provoked. They take themselves very seriously and have little patience for those who oppose them."

"What's the source of their strength?" Sam asked.

"Funny you should ask that, Sam. That's a very good question, the answer to which, I might add, is something that you should weigh carefully. Taking into consideration that most of their members come from wealth, it would appear that combined, they could buy whatever they want. But these people are too smart for that. No, their strength lies in their credo, 'Skulls above all else'. Believe me they really live by that. Right and wrong doesn't exist in a conflict with them. They close ranks real tight and then they use their combined, and let me say, considerable, influence and intelligence network to defeat a common enemy. Their ties, connections as it were, go deep my friend, very deep into the fabric of this country. But that's not really what makes them unique."

"You mean there's more?" asked a surprised Sam.

"Oh, there is much much more. The thing that makes them unique is that they know just how powerful they are, but don't delude themselves into thinking that they are invincible. That's a key ingredient and because they know they can be vulnerable they are always on guard. It is a very dangerous foe who knows his own weaknesses and does not deny them. Their actions may appear arrogant, but I'm here to tell you that any sign of arrogance is just that, appearances. They really take the saying 'Noblesse Oblige' {noble obligation} to heart. They believe that they are patriots and they truly believe that they, and only they, know what's best for this country. As far as they're concerned, it begins and ends with them. Put it all together, son, and you have a group that is almost unbeatable; and I stress almost." Arlen finished and waited for Sam's reaction. He could see the wheels in Sam's head turning. In Arlen's mind, Sam would have been the perfect son, surely the perfect person to take over the reins of his empire. It would have been a great time working with Sam, to bring him along to make Sam his heir.

Sally's untimely demise ended any hope of that happening. Arlen hoped that Sam understood the weight of his words.

Sam leaned back against his police cruiser, but still did not speak. Arlen had said a mouthful.

"There is a man named Nicholas Arrington, class of '27. He spends a lot of time in New Haven, is kind of the unspoken father figure to the members at Yale. Other alumni come and go, but Arrington is the main guardian, you might say. The specter of him is always there. Oh, and by the way, another esteemed alumnus is our very own governor. So don't take his confused act seriously. The man knows a great deal about what's going on. That's why he's the governor and by the way, watch out for his trusted right hand boy, Buckley."

Sam wiped his brow. All this information was starting to make him perspire.

"Wonderful," was all an exasperated Sam could offer.

Arlen let out a laugh. "Oh, come on now, Sam, it's not all that bad. Just be careful and stay wide-awake if you ever cross paths with these people. Remember, they don't bite if you don't. If you need to contact them, just show proper respect. Believe me, they'll do the same. Keep in mind that they know they can be vulnerable. That should work for you. Besides, it takes a lot to get them riled."

"And when they become riled?" Sam questioned.

"Better not to find out, son, better not to find out," Arlen advised.

"Thank you, sir, for this and the demonstration, it was very impressive," said Sam.

"It was meant to be more than impressive," said Arlen.

Sam looked puzzled.

"Just another ingredient to be added to the mix, Sam," said Arlen. "There's a lot going on around these parts. Add them all together and you have a real witches' brew. That dead professor stumbled onto something for sure and so did that policeman from over in Saybrook. I don't know what's going on, but I'll bet my life that all these military activities are tied to this. You just be careful. The Skulls may or may not be involved here, but my guess is that they're not the ones to be concerned about. It's just not their style."

"By the way, Sam, I hear your new lady friend is quite a looker, real smart, too. I'll bet that thrills Allison Tinsley no end."

Sam just stood there, speechless. "How on earth?" he asked himself. Finally, he was able to regain his composure.

Sam thanked Arlen once again, but not before Arlen made one final statement. "You never heard this from me, Sam. I deal with these people all the time and it is imperative that they trust me. I hope you understand."

Sam assured him of his confidentiality and headed home to check on Martha. He immediately put in a call to the Old Saybrook police department to see if they had discovered anything at Ethan's home. They informed him that they had not. In fact, to his complete disbelief, Sam learned that no one had even gone to the chief's home. Sam was beside himself. He made up his mind that after this whole mess was over heads were going to roll in Old Saybrook.

"I need your help," said Sam to a slightly surprised Martha. "No one has gone to Ethan's home to investigate, so I'm going over there right now. Will you come with me? It'll make it easier if two do the work."

"Are you sure you don't want someone from Ethan's own department to be in on this?" Martha inquired.

"Is it that you have a wicked sense of humor or are you bearing a grudge towards me?" answered Sam.

"Let's go," said Martha, who always seemed to understand Sam's sarcasm.

By now, the fog was really blanketing the whole area, especially the area closest to the shoreline. Sam cautiously made his way to Ethan's house and made sure that the area was secure. He gave Martha a pair of cloth gloves to use and together they began going through Ethan's study. There were at least three hundred books. They worked for about an hour searching through the volumes and keeping up a light but steady banter. Sam would occasionally look over in Martha's direction and marvel that she was so thorough. He concluded that the time she had spent with the police in New York had been time well spent. He was grateful that she could save him from using Saybrook's Finest. But then he noticed that she was silent. He looked over to her direction to see her staring at an open book.

"What have you found?" he asked.

Martha did not answer, but made her way over to Sam. She placed the open book in his hands. There were four pages of notes tucked neatly into the text. The notes revealed that Ethan happened to be in New Haven on a warm April evening when he observed a most unusual sight: a large group of young men, probably over one hundred, all wearing black hoods and capes, each carrying a lantern. It made for an eerie scene. Fascinated, Ethan inquired who they were and was told that they were the pledges of Yale's secret society. Most notable were the Skull and Bones, known on campus as the Skulls. He began researching them. Interestingly, the only name to appear in his notes was that of Nicholas Arrington. The notes further substantiated Martha's story from the night before. Sam had no way of tying the Skulls into his investigation because, truth be told, his investigation up to this very moment was a long list of questions with no answers. There had to be one common thread and now Sam was convinced that he had a starting place. For some reason he concluded that the death of the professor was the key to unlock all the other mysteries. Uncovering the reason why someone would kill Weiss was the key. Something kept telling Sam this was not a planned murder and it happened for an unrelated reason. It was a house of cards. Find the ace and everything else will fall into place.

After another hour of searching, Sam and Martha called it quits. They decided to go over to Nate's for coffee. When they pulled up to Zuckerman's they found the shop closed, but Bill Meechan was waving frantically from inside his hardware store. Sam and Martha went in. ·

"Where on earth have you been?" demanded Meechan. "Clara and your family have been trying to reach you for hours. They're holed up near Hamburg Cove trying to ride out the fog."

"Oh, my God, the kids," said Sam. "I completely forgot about them. Can I use your short wave?"

"Of course," said the owner. "It's in the back."

Sam made his way to the back room and put in a call to Injun Jim's boat. Satisfied the family was safe; he started to leave when he noticed two bullets on the floor near Meechan's workbench. He bent down and picked one up. It appeared foreign. He placed it in his pocket and joined Meechan and Martha.

"Thanks, Bill," he said, not making mention of the bullets. He and Martha went to Aunt Clara's to wait for Injun Jim to bring them safely back. He showed Martha the bullet, then called the police lab in Meriden and talked to Howard Grimes. Grimes was positive that the bullet was of German origin. That bit of information just added another question to the mix.

Dinner was an exciting occasion. The children had a great time up at Haddam and they shared a nautical adventure in the fog.

"Thomas swears he saw a pirate ship," said Mary. "Of course, none of us saw anything."

"I did, Dad, I really did," Thomas protested. "It was only for a brief second but I know I saw it. Injun Jim is going back first thing tomorrow morning to Hamburg Cove. You'll see, you'll all see," declared Thomas.

That evening, Sam, Martha, and the family walked up Main Street to the park. Nate Zuckerman was standing outside his store.

"Hope I didn't inconvenience you guys today," he said. "I just wasn't feeling very good so I closed up early. How about some ice cream and a fresh pot of coffee?" he offered.

Sam looked at the children's pleading eyes and accepted Nathan's offer. Aunt Clara just looked on with an amused smile.

"A real taskmaster, isn't he?" she joked to Martha.

"A beast," offered Martha in agreement.

It wasn't long before Bill Meechan came in, followed by the Peterson brothers who had just closed up shop. Peterson Brothers' auto repair was the largest property on Main Street, right next door to Meechan's. Not long after that, Wanda Loomis came over from the Black Swan followed by a few more of the locals. It was quite a gathering. Aunt Clara held court, much to Martha's amazement.

"There's just no end to this woman, is there?" Martha said fondly to Sam.

"She's really something, isn't she?" Sam responded.

Everyone was having a great time, but Sam could not take his eyes off Bill Meechan. Tomorrow, Mr. Meechan's life was going under the microscope.

CHAPTER 8

Sam had just downed his second cup of morning coffee when the phone rang. It was Howard Grimes.

"You're up early," said Sam.

"Actually, I'm still up," Grimes informed him, "I've got some news that should interest you." Without waiting for Sam's response, the medical examiner continued. "It's my conclusion that Ethan was shot at close range first, probably in a struggle. The second shot would not have been fatal. That leads me to believe that our killer was no marksman. He or she probably panicked and fired again as Ethan fell backwards. Of course, the shots came within seconds of each other, but my guess is that the first shot was the one closest. It probably means that the killing wasn't done in anger, not premeditated. Chances are it just happened."

The news was a relief to Sam who did not want to believe that one of his neighbors was a cold-blooded killer. It also was beginning to lend credence to Sam's gut feeling that the two murders were the result of some freak occurrence that set off a series of events that had gotten out of control for the killer. Sam was really starting to believe that he had found a starting place at last.

"I'm releasing the body, Sam," Grimes informed him. "The mayor over in Old Saybrook wants to hold the funeral as soon as possible. Ethan had no family, so the town is going to take responsibility for all the arrangements. It's time to lay Ethan to rest."

Sam agreed. "Thanks for working so fast on this, Howard. Ethan was a good man, and now you've given me a place to start. Whoever did this will not know a moment's rest, you can be sure of that," said Sam.

"I understand," said Grimes. "Call me if you need me, Sam, it's always good to hear from you, even if it's at times like this."

Sam hung up the phone and thought for a moment. Then he called the Rucker's and spoke to Marvin. He informed him that he was sure that Robert was completely innocent, but that he felt that the best place for Robert was in jail. First of all, he couldn't get into trouble there. Secondly, there would be very little chance to implicate Robert in the second shooting as well as any other that might occur. Both Weimer and the county prosecutor, Fine would be notified later that day of the coroner's findings in the death of Chief Taft. Fine would then have to make a decision whether or not Robert was part of the second killing. The newspapers were making a strong case that Robert was a dupe in all of this. The New Haven Register was weaving all sorts of tales of intrigue and clandestine operations by possible foreign agents. Sam told Marvin that he suspected Weimer's people had a large hand in this. Fine probably came to the same conclusion. The prosecutor would not be too happy to come out of this with egg on his face and he would be considering every angle to protect his reputation, to say nothing of his political future. In any case, Robert was better off right where he was for now. Marvin Rucker agreed with him. Marvin would tell the family, but would also heed Sam's advice to keep this to themselves. It probably wouldn't be long before Robert was released on bail, but he was still better off where he was.

Sam went over to tell Aunt Clara, who was having breakfast with Martha and the children. Aunt Clara received the news with great joy and praised the Lord.

"Ella Mae will be so relieved," she said. "I believe that you are one hundred percent correct, Sam, that fool son of hers stays put. Knowing that boy as I do, he'd most probably get drunk again and do something stupid. He's real good at that, you know. Nope, just let him sit in that cell as long as possible and give that family some relief."

Sam decided to have breakfast with everyone. It had been a while since they all had breakfast together and even though Sam was no closer to solving the crimes, he decided to take a brief pause and enjoy the first positive news he had experienced all week.

Everyone was in a good mood when Sam excused himself to go to work. He had some checking up to do on the local hardware store proprietor. If he was lucky, Meechan's fingerprints were on file with the state, making his task a little easier. Martha decided to take a walk into town while the children went fishing off the boat yard pier.

Martha walked up the east side of Main Street enjoying the window dressing of the local merchants. She stopped by Essex Antiques at the corner of Main and North Main. Some of the paintings on display really impressed her. She made her way over to the west side past Peterson Brothers' garage and Meechan's before noticing Wanda Loomis having coffee at Zuckerman's.

"Hey, Dearie," came Wanda's cheery greeting as Martha sat down next to her at the counter. Martha accepted Wanda's invitation to join her for a morning cup.

"I've drunk more coffee and eaten more food since I've been here than at any other period of my life. I swear I'm either going to blow up or develop a nervous condition; can't decide which," Martha said.

"Well, with that figure of yours, honey, I wouldn't be too concerned," said Wanda. "How are you doing?" she asked with a twinkle in her eye.

Martha knew that Wanda had her suspicions about her and Sam. After ten minutes with Wanda, Martha concluded that the whole town had plenty of ideas on that subject. Martha was just a little taken aback.

"Relax, cutie," advised Wanda. "This is a small town and everybody's got their nose in everyone else's business. Believe me, they'd make it up if it wasn't true. There's nothing like a nice juicy bit of gossip to make the time pass. This ain't exactly a bustling city in case you hadn't noticed. You just enjoy yourself and do whatever seems right to you. The Tylers are wonderful people and Sam, well, they don't come any better than that man." Then Wanda caught herself. "Oh here I go, just rambling on and on."

Nate finally piped in and agreed. All three shared a laugh. Martha escorted Wanda out and watched her as she crossed over and disappeared into the Black Swan. As she started to walk back down Main Street towards Aunt Clara's, she got an uneasy feeling. She sensed that an automobile was following behind her at a slow speed. As she turned to see who it was a large four door black Packard sedan sped ahead and then abruptly stopped. The right passenger door opened and out stepped Alison Tinsley. The Tinsley woman closed the door and stood in Martha's path. The women eyed each other, but neither spoke.

"Is there something I can do for you?" Martha asked, finally.

"Leave town and don't come back," answered Allison.

Martha smiled, but did not respond.

"Do you think that was funny, Miss Big City?" Allison asked, placing her hand on her hips.

"Is this how they do it in Dodge City?" Martha joked.

"You're not welcome here. You don't belong and you simply don't fit in. So why don't you go back to where you came from. You're out of your league," said Allison.

"What league is that, the junior league?" Martha said sarcastically. "I'm just guessing, but is that daddy in the car? So is he going to run me out of town?"

Just then, the mayor exited the Packard and took his daughter's arm. "Get back in the car, Allison," he ordered. "You're making a fool of yourself." With that, the mayor guided his daughter back into the vehicle. He looked Martha straight in the eyes. His gaze was not apologetic. He climbed back in and the Packard sped down Main Street then made a screeching left hand turn onto Griswald Square then to Pratt Street and North Main.

Now that they were gone, Martha noticed that she was shaking. Nate Zuckerman had been watching from his window and came over to see if she was alright. She assured him that she was, thanked him, and proceeded to Aunt Clara's house.

Aunt Clara was furious and was about to call the mayor to give him a piece of her mind. Martha stopped her. She knew how it felt to be on the outside of a relationship. Allison Tinsley had coveted Sam most of her life. Suitors had come and gone, but no one could ever measure up to Sam Tyler. With Sally gone and no one on the horizon, Allison just assumed that Sam would come her way after a respectable amount of time. Allison's problem was that she came across as a little too hungry, too aggressive. She had been a very good scholastic athlete in her younger years. Sam was just not attracted to that kind of woman. Martha knew that Allison Tinsley was no threat as far as she and Sam were concerned, but who could figure out what was going on in her head? Martha would keep her eyes open for Allison Tinsley. There was no telling what the woman was capable of.

Sam decided to do a background check on everyone who had access to Bill Meechan's store and back room. There was Nate, the Peterson's, Wanda and strangely enough, the mayor. Sam decided to call a friend in Washington to see if the F.B.I. or the Secret Service had any knowledge of these people. He knew that it was a huge shot in the dark, but what the heck, he might as well shoot the works, he had nothing to lose, or so he thought.

It was just after twelve noon that Sam received a call from James Buckley, asking him to meet at Sherman's Men's Club on the green in New Haven that afternoon. Buckley asked, but it sounded to Sam like the kind of request one doesn't turn down. Sam cleared his calendar and headed for New Haven. It took about an hour.

The Sherman's Club was all wood, chandeliers, and wall-to-wall money. Sam had been here before, but was never comfortable in the famous New

Haven "boys club". Sherman's Club was to New Haven what the Plaza at the turn of the Century had been to the elite of New York.

Buckley stood as Sam approached the table. An impeccably dressed, gray haired, deeply tanned gentleman was also there. He remained seated. Buckley shook Sam's hand, thanked him for coming on such short notice. He invited him to join them.

"This is Nicholas Arrington, Sam," said Buckley.

Sam and Arrington exchanged greetings. They all agreed that it was too late for lunch and too early for dinner. Sam settled for coffee while the two men ordered something a little stronger.

"How is your investigation going, Sam?" asked Buckley.

"I still have many more questions than I have answers, but we're beginning to turn the corner, I believe," said Sam.

Buckley informed Sam that Arrington was a businessman with companies in New York and New Haven.

Sam decided on a bold approach. "What else occupies your time in New Haven, sir?" he asked Arrington. Buckley and Arrington looked at each other. They were sure that Sam knew about Arrington's position with the Skulls. "James told me you were thorough," said Arrington. "It would have taken most policemen a great deal longer to be concerned with my people. I commend you. But let's get to the point, Captain. You, of course, know of my affiliation with a certain organization. A few well meaning politicians are trying to form some sort of connection between my organization and Nazi Germany. Of course, this is ridiculous, but nevertheless, we are not thrilled with the idea of the newspapers and some influential radio news people prying into our affairs. We prefer to be low key, in the background, so to speak."

Sam sat there showing total interest in Arrington's words. He offered nothing in the way of a response. Arrington became a little uneasy and felt the need to elaborate. "There are people ready to make a case for our involvement in the two homicides in your neck of the woods. I'm here to tell you that any looking in our direction will only make your job more difficult and take you farther afield. I can assure you that we have no knowledge of this matter, nor are we in any way involved. Weiss was certainly not one of us, and you can look from now to doomsday and you will not find any reason for us to associate with that pompous ass."

Sam looked down at his watch then addressed his two hosts.

"Its two-thirty, gentlemen. I called Washington at about ten o'clock this morning. Mr. Buckley contacted me at a little after noon. You people work fast. When did you find out that I called Washington and why would my calling be of interest to you? You certainly wouldn't know one of the people I was investigating, would you?"

Buckley started to speak but Arrington stopped him.

"Walter Tinsley is a school chum. We attended Choate together. Our families have been friends and associates for years. I've known Walter for thirty years. Trust me, the man is a weasel; he doesn't have the stomach for these messy goings-on. His family's money is his strength. He's inherited everything he has. He couldn't earn a dime out of politics. Believe me; I'm defending him solely to spare our families any disgrace. If he's implicated, he'll be ruined. He couldn't sell shoelaces if he had to. Our families are in business together. His disgrace is our disgrace. Look all you want, but you'll just be wasting your time and time is precious. All I ask is that you be fair with our people."

There was no mistaking the sheer arrogance of Arrington. This man held a lot of cards. Sam was not sure what was foremost on Arrington's mind: protecting the interest of his organization or blowing his own horn. It was obvious that this man was totally enamored of himself. He must really love his position as advisor to each succeeding class of the overblown elite.

"To put you at ease, sir, I would have to say that my belief at this moment is that if your organization is in any way involved, it is purely by accident. My investigation is taking me in another direction. I'm fairly confident that your people {Sam said 'people' with a question to make an impression on Arrington}, can rest well tonight."

Arrington grinned, knowing exactly what Sam was saying. "You're an Avon man, aren't you?" he asked.

"You've done your research, I can see," said Sam. "There is no need to send me any message, Mr. Arrington. I am well aware of what your people can do, what they are capable of. Right now, I have no interest in you. Please assume the same posture where I am concerned. Don't give me any reason to consider you, and I'll do the same."

Arrington got to his feet, a signal that this informal gathering was at an end. Buckley and Sam joined him. Arrington extended his hand to Sam.

"It has been a pleasure, Captain. The state is fortunate to have you on its watch. Hopefully we'll meet under more pleasant circumstances in the future."

Sam nodded and watched Arrington leave the room with great pomp and attitude.

"That wasn't pleasant," Sam quipped to Buckley who was still standing there.

"How do you manage to make these people like you?" he asked. "Arrington is very powerful, Sam, yet you handled him, and he didn't even mind. Very few people could pull off what you just did."

"It's a gift," returned Sam.

"Well, don't lose it, Captain, it's quite a gift."

Sam and Buckley left together. Buckley's driver was waiting to take him back to Hartford. Sam got into his cruiser and headed towards the Westbrook Barracks.

It was five a.m. when the phone next to Sam's bed started ringing. Sam found the receiver and asked who was calling.

"You've got to be kidding," he heard himself say.

The early morning crew at Saybrook Point Yacht Club in Old Saybrook just discovered the harbormaster dead in the marina waters. He had been shot in the head. Sam jumped out of bed, showered quickly, and drove down to Saybrook Point, sirens blazing.

The Saybrook Police had roped off the area as a crime scene. The harbormaster's body was lying covered on the dock and three uniformed officers were standing watch. It was the first professional conduct Sam had observed from them. Sergeant Michael Varnich, the desk sergeant, had taken control of the scene and was waiting to fill Sam in. Sam looked around and had to admit that the police presence was impressive.

"Well, Sergeant," he said as he approached, "looks as though you've done everything by the book. What have you got?"

"We have a male Caucasian, fifty-four years of age, dead in the water. One bullet wound, apparently inflicted to the back of the head at close range. It looks as though the shooting took place in the boathouse; there were signs that the victim fell over a workbench. We found blood on the workbench and on the floor; we assume it belongs to the victim. It appears he was dragged to the edge of the dock and thrown in there. We've got some more bloodstains over here but not much else. It will be up to the state forensics people to elaborate. I took the liberty to call them, sir; I didn't want anyone else involved. I hope that is alright with you."

Sam stood there looking at the sergeant as if he were dealing with a completely different person.

"Outstanding work, Sergeant," said Sam, and he meant it.

Sam went over to the body and observed the wound. The harbormaster was wearing his official windbreaker of the Saybrook Yacht Club.

"Sir, I'd like to speak with you if I may," said the sergeant.

Sam got up and directed him to go ahead.

"I know that our department got off on a bad footing with you sir, but I want you to know that we were emotionally unprepared for what was happening. Chief Taft was an outstanding police chief and he prepared us for this all right. I guess we just took him for granted, he was so damn good. He thought of everything, took care of everything; I think we were all stunned to find that something could happen to him. It was my responsibility as second in command to take charge and I failed to do that. Please don't hold the department responsible in any way. No one else had the authority to do anything, only me. I guess the chief's death was something I didn't want to believe could happen. We were very close. For the chief's sake, I would like to change your opinion of us if I can. The chief ran an A 1 police force and that is what you can expect from us from now on. I just don't want the next chief to think that he is taking command of some keystone cops. That's all I have to say, sir. We are just here to do whatever you feel is necessary."

Sam had to admit what the sergeant said made sense. It was true that nothing like this ever happened in these parts, especially the brazen murder of a police chief. Now there were three murders to deal with. It was a foregone conclusion that all three were related.

"I'm sorry if I was hard on you, sergeant," said Sam. "But it appears that you've got this situation well under control. I'm sure Chief Taft would approve."

"Thank you, sir, that's nice of you to say that," said Sergeant Varnich.

"I mean it," said Sam. "Thank you for doing such a professional job. I'm sure that the forensics people will appreciate such a clean crime scene."

Just then, the coroner's office and the state's chief medical examiner arrived on the scene. Sam and the sergeant stood by while Howard Grimes and his team did their work. It took a few hours and then they had the body transported to Meriden.

"I'll call you when I've got something," said Grimes.

Sam watched the examiner leave and turned to give final directions to the sergeant.

"I know it's going to upset a few members, but we'll have to keep at least this portion of the club closed to the public as a crime scene. I'll clear it with the mayor and get back to you before tonight. If you need me, call me," said Sam. He held out his hand and shook hands with the sergeant.

"You've done a good job here, sergeant," he said. "I'll be in touch."

Sam headed home to check on his family. Before he left the house this morning, he had called Aunt Clara to go over to look after the children. It was seven forty-five a.m. before he was able to get back. He was surprised to see Martha there too.

Sam made his hellos and went straight for the coffee pot.

"This thing is getting out of hand, Samuel," said a very concerned Aunt Clara.

Sam took a large gulp and sat down at the breakfast table with the women.

"Three brutal murders in seven days," moaned Sam. "If I don't start pulling this thing together," . . . he didn't finish the statement.

"I talked to Injun Jim yesterday," said Martha. "He went over to Hamburg Cove to check on Thomas's sighting."

"Did he come up with anything?" Sam asked.

"He didn't see anything resembling a pirate ship but what he did find might be of some help considering the murder at the Yacht Club," said Martha.

Just then, Injun Jim made his way up the stairs and knocked at the back door.

"Come on in Jim," said Sam. "Martha tells me you were over at Hamburg Cove yesterday. What did you find?"

"Well, I didn't find no pirate boat, but I did find something pretty interesting. First off, I went over every inch of the shoreline and found something real strange. There is a small inlet, well hidden by the overgrowth, but I found it alright. When I went into it, I found a small dock about a hundred feet in. Now a good size boat could make it there and out all right, and I found a small boathouse. I figured it was part of an estate so I poked around and found a few things. First off, there were signs that someone was there recently. Second off I walked up a ways and spotted a large house atop the hill. I checked when I got back and found that the Ryder family of New York abandoned the place. Guess they went belly up when the crash came."

"And the third?" asked Sam.

Injun Jim raised his hand and headed out the door. "Be right back," he said.

After a few minutes, he reappeared holding an oar. He used newspaper to make sure that his fingerprints would not conflict with anyone else's.

Sam jumped up to look at the place where Jim was pointing. There appeared to be blood on it. Sam took the oar, said goodbye and headed out the door. But he stopped, placed the oar carefully down, and reentered the kitchen. He walked over to Martha, bent over and kissed her. Aunt Clara and Injun Jim were just a little taken aback.

"I'll explain it to them," said Martha. "You just be careful and call me later."

Sam left and got into his car and headed up to Meriden. Aunt Clara and Injun Jim looked at each other and then over to Martha.

"Young lady, you've got some explaining to do. Something's been going on, right under my nose," bellowed Aunt Clara.

"More coffee?" asked Martha.

CHAPTER 9

Sam could not contain his feeling. This was certainly the longest of long shots, but Thomas might just have helped in a big way.

Howard Grimes was waiting for Sam and then took charge of the oar. "I can have prints, if there are any, in three hours. You know the blood will take more time. First off, I can tell you if it is human. Give me a day or two and I'll be able to tell you if the blood type matches up with the professor's."

"Fair enough," said Sam. "I'm going back to New Haven to go back over those cases Chief Taft was working on. I'll have my ear to the phone."

"You got it," said Grimes.

Sam called Martha to tell her that he was going to New Haven. He asked her if she wanted to visit her friend. Martha gladly accepted his invitation. Sam knew he could have gone straight down to New Haven, but he had to admit that he didn't want to spend the whole day without seeing Martha. It would give him a chance to discuss the case and get her take on things, but to be perfectly honest; he just wanted to be with her.

Once again, Sam made the ride shorter by the use of his siren and the ability to speed down to Essex. Martha had called Peter and Liz, who were overjoyed that she would be back so soon. Things were finally starting to come together and it felt good just to have Martha in the car with him.

Sam dropped Martha off at the Childers' residence and headed over to New Haven Police Headquarters.

Sergeant Donofrio already had a fresh pot of coffee waiting for Sam as he arrived. Sam spent the next few hours going over the files and found one that interested him. An unidentified man was found dead and his body dumped in the train yard just north of the city. The man carried papers that suggested he was of German ancestry, but no one was ever able to identify him. The murder case was seven years old and the victim considered an immigrant. Checks with the Federal Government agencies had no record of his existence. He had no known address nor did he have any papers or anything to suggest that he was from the area.

"Perfect," thought Sam. Germany was coming at Sam from all directions. It had to be the thread that pulled the whole tapestry together. Sam was sure of it. Now all he need do was prove it. Then he thought to himself, "a little luck wouldn't hurt."

Sam drove across town to meet Martha at the Childers' and Peter and Liz insisted on cooking their specialty, chicken cacciatore alla napolitana for Martha and Sam. The Childers belonged to a gourmet-cooking group of Yale professors and their spouses. The chicken dish was the one that Peter and Liz felt was their best and so they wanted to entertain Martha and her new beau with a nice relaxed home cooked meal. Once again, the evening went along well. Peter was on his best behavior and later he was more than willing to show Sam the residence of the Skull and Bones Society.

Sam felt that they should wait until after dark. At a little past eight-thirty p.m. the Childers directed Sam over to High Street and the famous secret residence of the Skulls. The first thing Sam noticed was the absence of any windows. The building appeared as a giant tomb with apparently only one entrance. The mood was dark and foreboding, certainly not very inviting. It was obvious from its outward appearance that the members wished to convey a strong message of secrecy and mystery. One could almost envision the words "Private, Visitors Not Welcome," inscribed in Latin above the entrance. In any case, Sam got their message. He also noted that Peter's behavior was one of excitement and fear while Liz's was just plain scared. Sam decided that Liz was the smarter of the two. He dropped the Childers off at their residence, thanked them, and with Martha in tow, headed back to Wolf Harbor. They had only traveled a few blocks when Sam guided the car into a vacant parking space between parked cars on a sleepy neighborhood street. Before Martha could inquire as to the reason, he gathered her in his arms and kissed her. Martha did not resist, but was a little surprised.

"I've wanted to do that all day," said Sam.

"Well, far be it from me to reject such a lovely gesture," was Martha's playful response as she pressed her body to his.

Once again, they embraced with mutual fervor, and then Sam reluctantly released her. He looked into her eyes, but said nothing; words weren't necessary. Martha knew exactly what he was thinking. Sam turned to take the wheel and proceed as Martha clung to him and kissed his neck, and then placed her head on his shoulder.

"I love when you kiss me," said Martha as Sam resumed the drive over to Route One. It wasn't until they reached North Branford, a good fifteen mile ride that one of them spoke. All the while, Martha never released her hold on him. This pleased Sam very much.

"Did you find what you were looking for?" asked Martha.

"Yes and no," was Sam's response. "I found out something that I think will be very helpful, but just like everything about this case, it opens a door but also presents a question."

"Tell me about it," said Martha.

"Well," Sam began, "there was an unsolved murder in the New Haven train yards around seven years ago. The victim was wearing German made clothing and had some papers in his possession written in German. An autopsy confirmed his western European origin, but nothing else. By the way, he was shot once in the back of the head, much the same way as our latest victim, the harbormaster. There was no way of finding out who he was, nobody claimed him, so the police had no choice but to rule it a John Doe homicide. I'm going to check with the chief medical examiner to see if the caliber of bullet and type of weapon are consistent. Once again, like everything else in this case, it is a long shot. It's not like I have a bunch of leads jumping out at me."

Martha did not respond. Something that Sam said caught her attention. The words "jumping out" for some reason gave her pause.

"What are you thinking?" asked Sam.

"You know, Sam, it's just like developing the story lines for my books," said Martha.

"You'll have to be a little more specific," said Sam.

"If we write down everything we know we can probably arrange things so that we might begin to establish a pattern. In any event, things might become a little clearer when they're all right in front of us. What do you think; want to give it a try?" Martha asked.

"I like it," said Sam. "We'll start as soon as we get back."

"Now just a minute there, Mister, it's going to be darn late when we get home." Martha protested.

Sam did not speak, but looked over to Martha, wearing a very wide grin.

"What, what's so amusing?" she asked.

"Home, you said back home," said Sam, but nothing more.

"How do you do that?" Martha demanded.

"Do what?" asked Sam.

"Hear that one word and shift the focus away from the subject to the word. You did that with Mary the day I met you. How do you do that?" Martha wanted to know.

Sam just laughed. "I have no idea how it happens. It just happens," he answered. "But I'll tell you what. We'll try your idea first thing tomorrow. Will that be alright?"

"That will be just fine, Mr. Tyler," cracked Martha. "I'm glad you know how to be civil."

Sam looked over in Martha's direction. "Well, are you going to stay all the way over there?" he wanted to know.

Martha did not answer, but slowly resumed her place close to Sam. They rode a little while longer in silence, and then Sam finally spoke. "I really love kissing you."

Martha and Sam were beginning to format a board of case occurrences when the phone rang and Sergeant Varnish informed Sam that Chief Taft's body would have a one day showing tomorrow, and the funeral would follow the next morning. The town of Old Saybrook wanted Sam to be among the many dignitaries at the service. Sam readily accepted and thanked the sergeant for the call. Sam put in a call to the mayor of Old Saybrook to thank him for including him in such a position of honor. They spoke for a few moments and then Sam came back to the kitchen to resume his work with Martha.

Sam took a moment to give his emotions a chance to calm down. He really missed Ethan and was upset that the case wasn't moving along more quickly. In other words, Sam was still getting nowhere. Martha leaned closer and gently stroked his hair.

"We'll get these people, Sam," she assured him. "I'm sure that Chief Taft knows you are doing your very best."

"I sure wish he'd give me a sign," Sam responded.

"Well, let's get started. Maybe he will," said Martha.

"Yeah, maybe he will at that," said Sam.

After twenty minutes, Martha and Sam laid out all the facts on the table and were able to categorize each one. Sam had to admit that any new information would probably begin to fill in some spaces, making the whole process move along more swiftly. He looked over at Martha who smiled back.

They were just about to call it quits when Sam received a call from Howard Grimes in Meriden.

"Well, my boy, I've got some good news and I've got some more good news. Which would you like to hear first?"

"Don't play with me, Howard, one more false hope and I'm liable to drive off Saybrook Point myself," quipped Sam. "How about more good news first," he joked.

"Good choice," said Grimes. The gun that killed Chief Taft was the same one used on the harbormaster. So that makes your German connection even stronger. The wood from the oar definitely matches what we got from the professor's skull. Safe bet that the blood matches up. And Sam, we got a partial print from the oar. We're checking it now with the F.B.I. This wouldn't by any chance be your birthday, would it?" joked Grimes. "Sam, are you there?"

Sam was speechless. All of a sudden, positive information was pouring in where none had existed since the case began. "I'm here, Howard," said Sam. It's just that it's about time we started to get something we can sink our teeth into."

"How on earth did you come up with that oar?" asked Grimes.

"Just plain dumb, wonderful luck," returned Sam. "I'll tell you all about it when I see you."

"That would be tomorrow in Old Saybrook," reported Grimes.

"Yeah, I guess you heard," said Sam.

"It's about time they laid Chief Taft to rest," said Grimes.

"I know," said Sam. "But I'd sure like to know what Ethan discovered that got him killed. No matter how you look at it, we've still got a killer in our midst down here."

"Patience, Sam, you'll get your man. Things are starting to come together."

Sam and Grimes signed off. Sam could not wait to tell Martha the good news and to fill in some more of the puzzle. They placed the information in its proper places and came up with two very strong scenarios. On one hand, there was the professor's murder, which seemed linked to Ethan's murder. On the other, there were the two murders of the chief and the harbormaster, both killed with the same gun. Robert Rucker was figuring less and less in all of this. Sam was totally convinced that an international incident just happened to occur in a small town. The biggest question remained how to link the first murder to the second two. Once again, the phone rang and once again, it was Howard Grimes.

"This must be your lucky day, Sam. If I were you I'd play the numbers today."

"What's up, Howard?" asked Sam.

"I had the boys down in New Haven send up all the ballistics files from that John Doe murder seven years ago. Well, guess what? The bullets and the weapon are a match. Whoever killed that man seven years ago also killed Chief Taft and the harbormaster. Whoever did this is one arrogant son of a bitch, my friend."

Sam thanked Howard for the news and went back into the kitchen. The word "arrogant" made Sam immediately think of Nicholas Arrington. As far as Sam was concerned, Arrington was the embodiment of arrogance. But could he be arrogant enough to kill four people? If Arrington was involved, could Mayor Tinsley be far behind? Oh, this was too good to be true.

"But I thought you said Tinsley was a weasel?" questioned Martha.

"No, Arrington said he was a weasel. I guess I know why he went out of his way to head me off. In any event, it's still only conjecture. I could be totally wrong, but I'm going to do some checking up anyway. What have I got to lose?" he asked.

"Let's take a ride," said Sam.

"To where?" asked Martha.

"I was thinking like Saybrook Point. There's a really good seafood restaurant right on the Point."

"And so near the Yacht Club to boot," countered Martha.

"I knew you were more than a pretty face," said Sam.

"Flattery will get you everywhere, Mr. Tyler," said Martha. "Let's go, I'm famished."

"We just ate breakfast a few hours ago," protested Sam.

"It must be the . . . ."

"Air," said Sam before she could finish. "I think I've heard that before."

About halfway to Old Saybrook Sam got yet another call from Chief Medical Examiner Grimes.

"My God, you'll probably be taking a vacation after this case," kidded Sam.

"Nobody knows the sacrifices I make for the State, Captain," came Grimes right back.

"What have you got?"

"Try and stay on the road but we actually got a name from the print on the oar. The print belongs to Joseph Menger. The police down in New Haven had him on file. It seems he was arrested in a protest riot at Yale in '33." No one has seen him since. He appears to have vanished about that time."

Sam thanked Howard and proceeded to Saybrook Point. Saybrook Seafood at the Point was a large wooden structure featuring fresh catch of the sea daily by the local fishermen. The Point offered a perfect view of the mouth of the Connecticut River flowing into Long Island Sound. Martha enjoyed her fish and chips, but the setting really pleased her.

"I never realized such a beautiful place as this existed," she said. I've totally fallen in love with this area, Sam."

"So much that you could live here?" Sam asked, surprised that what he was thinking managed to come out of his mouth. "I'm sorry, that wasn't fair. I shouldn't press you."

"Oh, I disagree," said Martha. "I think that we should definitely discuss it. I certainly don't want things hanging in the air. And I really would like to know what your thinking is."

"You said it yourself, you're fast lane and I'm country lane," said Sam.

"I also said that I'm really beginning to enjoy the country lane," countered Martha. "I've given this some thought and I really believe that we can work it out."

"What about your teaching position?" asked Sam.

"Well, I was going to wait a little while before telling you, but Peter actually made me an offer to fill a vacant position at Yale. It's just what I want because I don't want to be tied down to a full teaching load anymore, and this job is just perfect for my needs. Besides, I don't need the money. My writing has afforded me a wonderful income. I would be free to do the lecture circuit, which I have always wanted to do. So you see everything is just perfect, except . . . ."

Sam gave Martha a puzzled look. "I'm missing something," he said.

"No, actually it is I who am missing something. I just felt that it was way too soon to expect some sort of commitment from you." "That," she said with heavy emphasis on the word 'that,' would not be fair."

Sam had to admit he was in troubled waters.

"Look, Sam, I told you the other day that I wasn't expecting anything. I just want you to know that I love you. I've never been more sure of anything in my life. I'm not some young schoolgirl and I fully appreciate your position. You have far more to be responsible for than me. I could not blame you for taking the slow route. But I want you to know that I've found something here that is very precious and I would not miss it for the world. Too many people are just too damn scared to take a leap of faith, but that is not going to happen to me. When I look at your children, I can see their mother. Remember I'm a writer, but I'm also a woman. Sally must have been wonderful, and I'm so sorry you lost her. I love you enough to say that. But I'm also old enough to know my own mind. I wasn't just talking the other evening when I told you that I cannot get enough of you. I just want to be a part of your life and that includes the children, Aunt Clara and anyone else, for that matter. Remember Ellen and I are already friends. As I said, I think we can work this out. What do you think?"

Sam just sat for a moment. He was more interested in savoring Martha's words than attempting to match them.

"You're sure?" he asked finally.

"Dead sure, Mister," said Martha with total conviction.

Sam got up and walked over to the bar area. Martha didn't know what to think as she observed Sam talking to a large gentleman at the bar smoking a cigar. She noticed Sam give the man money and then the two shook hands. Sam turned and walked back to their table.

"What was that all about?" Martha asked.

Sam reached across the table and took Martha's left hand. He placed his hand in his coat pocket and produced a cigar band. He placed the paper wrapper on Martha's finger. Martha was in shock.

"It's a little big and just a little flimsy, but all you have to say is 'yes' and I'll replace it with the real thing."

Martha for once was speechless.

"For someone who had a whole mouthful to say just a few minutes ago, you're awfully quiet," said Sam.

"You're sure?" asked Martha.

"Dead sure," said Sam, with equal conviction.

Sam noticed a tear rolling down Martha's face. Neither of them could say anything.

"You're right," said Sam, after a few moments. "We can work it out."

Sam leaned over and kissed Martha.

"Let's get out of here," he said. They got up and headed for the exit. When they reached the parking lot, Sam had one more question for Martha.

"You really have a lot of money?" he joked.

"Tons," answered Martha back.

"Good, cause if we don't crack this case I'll have to apply for a job out of law enforcement. Who in the world would hire me?"

Sam did not wait for an answer. They got into the car and headed out.

"While we're here why don't we make a quick visit to the Yacht Club?" suggested Sam.

"What a novel idea," countered Martha, knowing Sam's intentions all along.

One minute later, they were pulling up to the main building of the Harbor One Yacht Club.

Sam exited the vehicle and came around to open Martha's door. They walked the long pier to the area where the harbormaster's body was found. Sam spoke to the officer on duty and learned that no new evidence had materialized. Once again, he inspected the crime scene. Early on in his career, Sam realized that each crime scene had its own story and if you really cleared your head and listened, he swore the crime scene would reveal its secrets. A good practice was to try to envision the crime as it happened while allowing your powers of observation to click in. The more you looked, the more your mind would register all the nuances of the scene. Sometimes you could draw an instant conclusion and at times, others would come later. Sam was beginning to get the feeling that this was one of those later times. Martha knew enough not to trespass on the crime scene unless invited. As this was still an official crime scene, Sam could not invite her in.

"Find anything?" Martha asked.

Sam gave her a look that said, "I should be so lucky."

"While we're here, could we take some time to look at all these lovely boats? God, some are amazing," said Martha.

"Sure," said Sam. "I'm sure that would be alright with the people in charge. We could lie and say we're investigating. No one would be the wiser."

"I wish I had worn something a little more police business-like to give our story a little more credibility," said Martha, who was wearing a lightly colored skirt and blouse ensemble accented by a pair of bone colored sandals.

"I think you look just great the way you are," said Sam, choosing to address the way Martha looked over that of proper investigation attire.

Martha took his hand and led him down the large section of the pier marked "private members only."

"One boat is bigger and more beautiful than the rest," Martha observed.

"Yeah, and more expensive," quipped Sam. "There's a lot of wealth tied up in these waters."

Martha nodded in agreement and walked with Sam among the many majestic wooden vessels. Just then, Sam caught sight of something odd. There among the multitude of luxurious ladies of the sea, Sam came face to face with the smallest, ugliest sailboat he had ever seen. The body of the vessel could not even measure more than fifteen feet or so. It had a large mast and a square, nondescript cabin. There wasn't room for much more. It was painted blue, bearing a white dock.

Sam commented on it to the assistant harbormaster. The man just laughed.

"I know the boat well," he said. "Kinda sticks out like a sore thumb, don't you think?" he asked.

Sam and Martha had to laugh. The man's observation was right on target. It truly did stick out like a sore thumb.

Without asking him, the man looked through the logbook and located the boat and its owner. "That one there is definitely a home-made job, no boat builder builds anything like that," he informed Sam and Martha. Belongs to a Joseph Menger," he said.

"What name did you say?" asked Sam as if not believing his own ears.

"One Joseph Menger," reported the man. "Doesn't come around much, though," he continued. "Pays for all the docking and storage charges, even the necessary maintenance, but I've never seen him. As I said, doesn't come around too often."

"What is it, Sam?" Martha asked. "You look like you've seen a ghost."

"Maybe I have," Sam returned. He took Martha in tow, thanked the assistant harbormaster, and headed for the car.

"Joseph Menger disappeared from Yale seven years ago. He's the very same man that Howard Grimes called me about on our way down here. I think it's time for me to sit down with our illustrious governor and Mr. Buckley and get a few matters cleared up. But it will have to wait until after Ethan's funeral."

Clara Tyler's home exploded with joy as Sam and Martha broke the news of their engagement to Aunt Clara and the children. Lillith ran to Martha, threw her arms around Martha's legs and held on for dear life. Mary and Thomas went to their dad. The three of them took chairs at the kitchen table.

"Well, what do you think?" Sam asked his two oldest.

"Oh Daddy, we're so happy for you," said Mary. "Now we'll be a whole family again."

Sam was touched, but had some concerns. "You won't feel threatened by Martha, will you, Mary?" asked Sam. "I mean, it's not like she'll be taking your place," Sam assured her.

"Don't worry, Dad, I could use some help around here. Lillith is growing up and Thomas is beyond incorrigible," Mary said.

Everyone laughed at that, everyone except Thomas of course.

"Oh, brother," said Thomas with a tone of exasperation.

"As usual, Thomas has so much to say," Mary added sarcastically.

"Oh Mary," said Lillith, still holding onto Martha, "leave Thomas alone. You're always picking on him."

"Well, just another cozy evening with the Tyler Clan," remarked Aunt Clara.

"I'm so happy for both of you," she said. "It will be nice to have a woman in Sam's house again. Sam, I'm really happy for you and Martha. Well, what can I say? It hasn't taken you very long to make your way into our hearts."

Aunt Clara walked over to Martha. "Welcome to our family, my dear," she said as she embraced Martha.

Such an outpouring of affection moved Martha. Everyone loved the Tylers and now she was going to become one of them. Just a little more than two weeks ago, she had left New York in despair, and now her whole world had taken on new meaning. She looked down and saw that Lillith was still holding onto her.

"Let's keep this our little secret until I can put a real ring on Martha's finger, but I really think that we should celebrate and go out for dinner." Everyone agreed. Sam called Wanda Loomis and reserved a table at the Black Swan. As the family walked up Main Street, Sam filled Aunt Clara in on all that was happening with the case. Aunt Clara was overjoyed to hear that things were really looking quite good for Robert Rucker.

The family spent a very pleasant evening at Wanda's place. Wanda loved it when they came in for dinner. She really had great affection for the Tylers and went out of her way to ensure their satisfaction. Lillith, who insisted on sitting next to Martha, was beaming during the whole time. Finally, she leaned over to tell Martha something in secret.

"Now I'm going to have my very own mommy," she said.

Tears immediately came to Martha's eyes. "Oh yes, you are," she told Lillith. "And I'm so happy that it's me," she said as she leaned closer to kiss Lillith on the head.

"Me too," said Lillith.

Sam took the whole scene in. He had to admit that he never imagined he would see the day when something as wonderful as this would happen. But now it had, and he was having a hard time containing his excitement. He looked over to Aunt Clara who was all smiles. She gave him a nod of approval. That gesture said it all.

CHAPTER 10

Ethan Taft's funeral was a solemn affair attended by many dignitaries and representatives from numerous police forces from New Haven to Stonington on the State line. The absence of the governor and the attorney general, who sent representatives, made Sam's blood boil. He wasn't too happy with those two in the first place, but their absence was a slap in the face to a man who was respected and loved by many and who had given his life to preserve the law in the State of Connecticut. This case had drawn great media attention, and with so many watching, such a glaring absence was unforgivable. He made up his mind to share his feelings with both men as soon as he could arrange an appointment.

That night, the Tylers spent a quiet evening at Aunt Clara's. Ethan Taft was finally laid to rest. The finality was beginning to sink in for Sam. Never again would he and his old friend get together to shoot the breeze, laugh, and joke about the local politicos who always took themselves so seriously. Ethan was one of the few people who understood Sam. He really liked Sam's dry sense of humor. Ethan was a man of few words. He always felt that Sam could articulate the things he was thinking, but never felt the need to express. And now, Ethan was gone. It appeared as though Martha came into Sam's life at just the right moment.

The telephone was ringing as the family filed into Aunt Clara's. The children were making so much noise that they almost missed the call. Aunt Clara rushed over and picked up the receiver mid-ring.

"Well, how you doin', you sweet thing?" said Aunt Clara, while everyone looked on. "I guess you're just too important to visit family way up here. Probably be embarrassed by our country ways and all," she kidded the person on the other end. "She sure is, but you think long and hard, young lady, about coming on up here and visiting with us. You know we'd just love having you and that big shot husband of yours come stay with us. We sure have enough room."

With that, Aunt Clara motioned to Martha that the call was for her. "You take care now," were Aunt Clara's final words.

"Ellen, how are you?" asked Martha, recognizing Ellen's distinctive raspy voice. Martha listened for a few minutes while Ellen explained the reason for her call.

"You've got to be kidding," shouted Martha. "How much?" she asked.

Martha let out a loud scream. Then she and Ellen began a ten-minute exercise in girl talk. Sam led the family to the back porch to allow Martha her privacy. When Martha finally emerged from the house, it was obvious that the news from New York was all good.

"Okay, let's have it," said Sam. "It sounded like cousin Ellen was the bearer of glad tidings."

"Oh, Sam, you have no idea. It couldn't have come at a better time."

"Well, don't keep us in suspense," said Aunt Clara.

"Ellen sends her love to you and the children, Sam," Martha began. "The reason she called is to inform me that Harcourt wants to sign a five book deal worth a great deal of money. Ellen was able to get them in a bidding war with another publishing company. My contract with them was about to expire and both were anxious to sign me."

"I guess you weren't joking when you said you were a woman of independent means," kidded Sam.

"The sales of my books have grown steadily, each outperforming the previous one. To a publisher that's gold. There aren't too many publishers who can compete with Harcourt, but dear cousin Ellen drove the price for my signing through the roof. I could just kiss her. Sam, with royalties and screen rights, I won't ever have to worry where my next meal is coming from. Boy, are you the lucky one," Martha kidded Sam.

"Well, Aunt Clara," said Sam. "I guess we're set for life."

"That's pretty much how I see it," added Aunt Clara.

"There's just one problem," said Martha, sobering the mood.

"Here it comes," said Sam.

"Oh don't be silly, it's just that I have to go to New York tomorrow to meet with the publishers and my lawyer to sign the papers. It won't take long. Ellen has already worked out all the details with my attorneys. It's just a formality, but I must be there."

"How long will it take?" asked Sam.

"If I go on an early train tomorrow, I could be back by late afternoon the next day," said Martha.

"Overnight," declared Sam.

Martha hesitated. She looked to the whole family whose faces were suddenly solemn.

"I told Ellen that I would get right back to her," Martha said.

"What do you mean?" Sam asked.

"Well, I couldn't go without discussing it with you first," she declared.

Aunt Clara smiled, folded her arms and leaned back into her chair. It was obvious that Martha's decision to consult family first pleased her. Martha's actions made it obvious to her that Martha's commitment to Sam and the family was real and complete. Aunt Clara was indeed most pleased, and Sam took notice of that. To say the least, he was quite pleased himself.

"You promise to come right back?" pleaded Lillith.

"Wild horses couldn't keep me away for one second longer. Besides, young lady, you and I have lots to talk about. We've got to get you prepared for school this year. There are lots of clothes and supplies to buy. I'm thinking that a family shopping trip is about to be planned. What do you three say?"

The children exploded in agreement.

"I have to talk it over with your father first, but I have some ideas that you might like."

Sam could tell by the children's reaction that any attempt on his part to withhold agreeing would be like fighting a losing battle.

"Okay, okay," he said, above the children's shouts. "One more female vote added to the Tyler family. I can see where this is leading," said Sam, in mock despair. "Come on, gang, it's time for bed," he declared. "You might as well call Ellen and tell her you'll be there tomorrow," said Sam to Martha. "I'll tuck the kids in and then maybe you could join me for a little chat."

Martha called the children and then went to the hallway to telephone a waiting Ellen Gold.

Sam put the children to bed and waited for Martha to join him on the back patio. Martha quickly finished her business with Ellen, and then paused to spend a few minutes talking with Aunt Clara.

"This family is sure lucky you came along, young lady," Aunt Clara declared. "Sam's growing responsibilities with the state police and the raising up of the children was starting to pose a real problem around here. I just love helping Sam out, the kids are wonderful, but I'm not the person they need.

Martha, I hope that you'll be happy with your decision. There is nothing more important in life than family and here you are with one ready-made just dying to have you become part of it. I hope you realize just how fortunate you are, my dear. Becoming a Tyler is something considered very special around here. I just want you to know how pleased I am that things worked out the way they have. But just so we understand each other, I want you to be aware that I was a might skeptical at first. But I'm a pretty good judge of character and my guess is that we're darn lucky to have you. So give us a hug and let's start thinking about some wedding plans. The two of you living in separate homes makes no sense at all."

Martha hugged Aunt Clara with a force that caught Aunt Clara by surprise. But it felt good. Both women stopped crying and then they started to laugh uncontrollably.

"Now stop that," ordered Aunt Clara. "You'll get your face all swollen. We can't have your man see you looking like that."

Martha wiped away her tears. "Thank you, Aunt Clara," she said. "You have no idea what this means to me. I won't disappoint you or the family. I know that everything I want in life, everything I need, is right here with this family, my family. I know how blessed I am, believe me."

"Your man is waiting on you," said Aunt Clara. Go to him."

Martha backed towards the door then burst through it. She had to try to stop herself from running across the lawn. She felt like a young schoolgirl. Even when she was a teenager, Martha never experienced what she was feeling now.

Sam was waiting on the patio with a glass of iced tea for each of them. Martha collapsed in her lawn chair still smiling uncontrollably.

"Before you get too comfortable, Lillith wanted me to tell you that she wants you to come up to see her. Trust me, she won't fall asleep until you do."

Martha jumped up and quickly made her way to Lillith's second floor bedroom. She knocked and gently opened the door to see Lillith sitting up on her bed and waiting. Martha made her way over to Lillith's bed and sat down on it. The room's only illumination was a small pink table lamp with a lampshade. Even with such limited light, Martha was able to see the walls covered with paintings depicting Lillith's favorite fairytale characters: Little Bo Peep, Little Miss Muffet, as well as Raggedy Ann and Andy, all in attendance, surrounding Lillith.

"Well, Lillith, I'm certainly glad you waited up to see me. I was hoping we could talk before you went to sleep," said Martha.

"Oh, Martha, I can't wait for us to go shopping. Now I'll be able to shop with my very own mommy, just like the other kids. Can we go real soon?" asked a very anxious Lillith.

"Your daddy and I are going to talk about that. I'm sure it won't be long," Martha assured her.

They chatted for a few moments and Martha tucked Lillith in. It was the first time that Martha experienced the pure joy of putting your child safely to sleep. Later she allowed herself to hope that there would be many more nights of such peace and contentment. She remembered that as a child, her mother would always read to her and see her settled peacefully into dreamland. But as she got older, her mother grew cold, distant, into a world of intellectualizing and sterile deportment. She hadn't thought of such things in years. She made a solid vow never to allow that to happen between herself and Lillith, or the other children, for that matter.

Sam was sipping his iced tea under the stars, waiting for Martha's return.

"Everything alright?" he inquired.

"Perfect," said Martha with a smile.

"So, it looks as though my cousin is one sharp cookie," said Sam.

"You better believe it," Martha reassured. "New York Publishing is shark infested waters, but that cousin of yours can hold her own with any of those delusional peacocks."

"I detect a great sense of affinity for the peacocks," said Sam with his characteristic sarcasm.

"Some of those gentlemen, shall we say, are pretty full of themselves. It's such a pleasure to watch Ellen wrap them around her little finger. They never know what hits them until the aftershock. And her husband, the illustrious Paul Gold, is just putty in her hands. Trust me, if he ever cheated on her like so many of those big shots do, he'd be selling pencils in the Grand Central Station before she got through with him," declared Martha.

Suddenly, the area became very quiet. Sam looked over at Martha who had a strange look on her face.

"What is it?" asked Sam.

Then he realized what was on Martha's mind. "Are you sending me some sort of message?" he inquired.

Martha spoke not a word; instead, she got up and seated herself in Sam's lap. She put her arms around him and looked him square in the eye.

"Forget all that big city bologna, Mr. Tyler, let me tell you something right now. No woman but me had better ever come near you or sparks will really fly. And that goes double for that Allison Tinsley. Believe me, that will be one situation where even her daddy won't be able to help her," said a very determined Martha.

Sam pulled Martha to himself. He placed her head on his shoulder.

"I take my vows very seriously," he spoke gently to her. "Only death could come between us, Martha Frost. I can't wait for the day that I can call you Mrs. Tyler," he assured her.

Martha waited to speak, choosing to rest in the comfort of Sam's strong arms. Finally, she pulled back and spoke. "Oh Sam, I'm going to miss you and the children so terribly. It's too soon for me. I've grown so accustomed to spending each day with all of you that I can't bear the thought of being separated, even for one day."

Sam shifted his body and placed his hand in his pocket. He pulled it out and took hold of Martha's left hand. Slowly he began to slide a ring onto Martha's finger.

"Oh, my god," gasped Martha. "Oh, Sam, oh Sam," she said repeatedly.

"This was my mother's," he said. "When my parents first got engaged, my father gave her a very modest ring. After he made his fortune, he bought her this one. My mother wore it all her life, but told Aunt Clara that when she's buried, she wanted to wear the original ring. It had a great sentimental value for her. Aunt Clara never forgot. She's kept this for me all these years. I never gave her the opportunity to use it in my first marriage. But now, it seems only fitting that you wear it. The only woman I'll ever want is the one who wears this ring."

With that he kissed Martha with a kiss bearing as much conviction as it did passion and love.

Both agreed that they should be married as soon as possible. There would be a great party on the lawn following a service by Reverend Foster. It would be short notice, but Sam was sure that the truly important invitees would find a way to be there. Sam sensed that he was not too far from solving the murders at hand. Martha's publishing deal would ensure her ability to carry on her work away from New York. Things seemed to be really coming together for them. Still, Sam always experienced a hearty reserve that prevented him from getting ahead of himself. Once again, he reminded himself about the ongoing case. "A little luck couldn't hurt."

Sam saw to it that Martha got on the 9:14 out of Old Saybrook headed to New York. The family had an early breakfast at Aunt Clara's to see Martha off. It was obvious that no one, including Martha, wanted her to leave. The train slowly picked up steam before it gathered full speed towards New Haven and then New York.

It was a lonely tear-filled journey of two and three-quarter hours. It took about ten minutes into the ride for Martha to be convinced that she never again wanted to be without Sam and the children. There was no first class on this train, only coach. Martha never noticed.

The 9:14 pulled into Grand Central Terminal precisely on schedule, 12:01 p.m. Martha made her way through the crowds to the great floor. The crowded terminal, once a source of excitement and life to Martha, now seemed strangely annoying. The peace and serenity of Wolf Harbor had gotten more into her system than she had imagined. Martha made her way to the ladies' bathroom to try to repair her tear-damaged face. Mercifully, her face wasn't swollen, but her makeup was a mess. "Send in the tarmac," she thought to herself. She was to meet Ellen at Sardi's, New York's famous theatre restaurant at 12:30 p.m. "Just enough time for a major overhaul," she silently quipped.

"I'm sorry, did you say something, my dear?" asked an elegantly dressed elderly lady whom Martha had not even noticed standing next to her.

Martha had to laugh. "Oh, I'm sorry. I seem to be having a lot of conversations with myself lately. I hope I didn't disturb you."

The woman started to say something, but stopped herself abruptly and looked quizzically at Martha.

"Oh my," she exclaimed. "You're Martha Frost, aren't you?"

The woman went to shake Martha's hand, and then ran out of the public toilet babbling something to herself. Within a few seconds, she reappeared dragging two more expensively dressed friends behind. The women all began speaking at once, having reached the conclusion that this was, indeed, Martha Frost. It took a good five minutes for them to satisfy themselves and finally leave Martha to the problem at hand: redoing her face. The women went off to a matinee performance at the theatre. Martha completed her task, made her way out of the building on the 42nd Street side, and took a taxicab to Sardi's.

Ellen saw her enter, got up out of her seat and waved to Martha. Choosing Sardi's to meet was a token of great recognition of success. The hallowed restaurant had gained its reputation as the place where theatre people gathered to read the first reviews of their Broadway works. The parties after the reviews were that of great celebration or merciful commiseration. The caricature-lined walls bore the loving likenesses of the entertainment elite. Martha had always treasured the offering of a skinny, crooning Frank Sinatra. She had no idea why, she simply loved it.

Martha and Ellen hugged and took their seats. The waiter was already there to offer them drinks. Ellen chose scotch on the rocks with a twist and Martha ordered iced tea. The waiter wrote it down and vanished.

"Iced tea! That's Aunt Clara's favorite. Don't tell me my dear aunt has gotten to you. Who on earth celebrates a deal of this magnitude with iced tea?" Ellen demanded.

"Let's just say I want to keep my wits about me. I don't want to appear light-headed before such an august group as our publishers," said Martha.

Ellen accepted her reason, for now. She spent a few moments going over the deal with Martha. Both women ordered cobb salads. No sense feeling too filled up. This was not a time to become sluggish.

As they dove into their salads, they segued into good old-fashioned girl talk

"Tell me everything about your stay," demanded Ellen. "You look so damned refreshed, I hardly recognized you."

It was true, even though Martha had been crying. The two previous weeks at Wolf Harbor had transformed her from a frazzled mess into a woman exuding calm and coolness. Ellen had quickly taken notice.

"You never mentioned Sam," said Martha matter of factly.

"Oh, I figured you'd see him sooner or later. Sweet, isn't he?"

"And the children, somehow you neglected to mention them, also. How is that?" asked Martha.

Ellen had to own up to her omissions. "Let's face it. I had to present you with a tranquil picture for your own good. With that overactive mind of yours, who knows what you would have thought had I told you about my handsome state policeman cousin and his three adorable children who just happen to live right next door. Now admit it, you never would have gone."

Martha knew that she was right, but was not about to concede anything yet. She was going to have her fun at Ellen's expense.

"You also neglected to tell me that the children practically lived in Aunt Clara's house or that your cousin was so bright and sophisticated, to say nothing of the fact that he is a widower, and what a surprise, eligible."

Ellen immediately began to protest her innocence. Martha was having great fun. Somewhere in between Ellen's protestations, Martha managed to interject the words "and one hell of a kisser."

That comment stopped Ellen in her tracks.

"Wait a minute, wait a minute," she shouted. "Did you just say that Sam is a hell of a kisser?" she asked.

Martha just sat there, smiling.

"You mean that my cousin kissed you? Was it really good?" she wanted to know.

"You bet it was," said Martha.

"You snake," Ellen exclaimed. "What did you do?"

"I kissed him right back," she proudly proclaimed.

Ellen sat back in her chair, too stunned for words.

"Well, don't stop now," she managed, finally. "What the hell happened next?"

Martha didn't answer, but casually extended her left hand in Ellen's direction. At first, Ellen did not see it but when Martha asked that she pass the salt Ellen came face to face with Martha's diamond engagement ring.

"Ahh," Ellen screamed as she dropped the saltshaker and grabbed Martha's hand. By now, the lunch crowd was looking at them.

"She's engaged to my cousin!" exclaimed Ellen.

The restaurant crowd broke into applause. Many of the patrons knew both women. Some came over to offer congratulations. When everything had settled down once again, Ellen found herself staring at a woman she had become great friends with and now, through some magical transformation, was a complete stranger.

"You're going to live in Essex, aren't you?" she asked. I'm totally dumbfounded. This is just not happening."

"Oh, Ellen, how can I ever thank you? I was always a fish out of water here. I could never make the right decisions living here. This city is just so big, so overwhelming. I'm just a small town girl at heart. The only times I ever enjoyed here were when I was holed up in my apartment writing, or my time with you. Everything else was just a chore. I never really fit in here. There, I'm alive. The children bring out the best in me. And Sam, he completes me. I've got it all worked out. For the first time in my life, my life makes sense. I owe it all to you. If you hadn't tricked me, I don't know what would have become of me. I have to admit, I was at the end of the line. Now, I'm totally revitalized."

At that, Martha started to tell Ellen about the book she was putting together about all that was happening in Wolf Harbor. Ellen, fascinated by Martha's words, glanced at the clock on the wall and realized that they were in danger of being late for their appointment. They jumped up, paid the bill and ran to the street to hail a cab to the offices of Harcourt Press.

CHAPTER 11

As Sam made his way through the streets of Hartford, the city Mark Twain called "the most beautiful city on the face of the earth," he still hadn't reached a decision regarding a strategy with which to confront the governor. All he knew was that he was mad at the governor and James Buckley for their obvious slight to the memory of Ethan Taft. He decided to take a bold frontal approach. Sam was usually wise enough to know that he was not at his best when in this frame of mind. But time was not on his side so he was throwing discretion and caution to the wind.

Sam was ushered into the governor's chambers at the State House, a large grey stone building set in the middle of a majestic lawn that encircled it. It was high on a hill holding a commanding presence in the landscape. Both the governor and Buckley sensed that Sam's visit was not going to be friendly.

It didn't take Sam long to reveal the nature of his visit. He informed his two superiors of his disappointment at their disgraceful absence from Ethan's funeral. This startled both men, but Sam was only beginning. Next, he told the governor that no amount of power wielded by any secret society, no matter what the magnitude of their influence, would save Mayor Tinsley, if he or their organization were involved.

The governor finally erupted at Sam's words. He jumped to his feet yelling, "Just who the hell do you think you are, coming in here?" he demanded. "You would do well to tread softly, Captain Tyler. You are on my turf here so don't you forget it. Maybe you are forgetting who you're speaking to, but I am the damn governor, sir, and I can make life pretty miserable for you if you provoke me," frothed the governor.

"I am a public servant, sir, just like you," Sam returned with quiet venom. I am paid to look after the best interests of the people of the State of Connecticut, just as you are. And don't presume to threaten me. My family was here long before you came along. And we will be here long after you are gone. Threatening me doesn't exactly make me too well inclined to think that the interests of the people are your primary motivation."

Before things got too out of hand, Buckley jumped into the fray.

"Gentlemen, gentlemen, please let's calm down here. Nothing's going to be accomplished like this. Sam, we're sorry about Chief Taft's funeral, but the governor simply could not leave Hartford yesterday. Neither of us could leave. You'll just have to believe me on this, Sam. I wouldn't lie to you. It was only at the last minute that we decided to send some people to represent us. I'm deeply sorry for not informing you, but we could not leave. I can't go into detail, but going to Old Saybrook was not an option for us. The governor has decided to issue a proclamation for Chief Taft. His name will be entered on the scroll of meritorious honor, Sam, one that Chief Taft deserved. Our absence yesterday was not that of neglect. We were serving the interests of the people, for which you so rightly observed, is what we're paid to do. We were simply doing our job, Sam. As for Tinsley, let me say this. If he is involved in any of this, you have our blessing in bringing him to justice. The society to which you eluded officially declares no partaking in any of this. If Mayor Tinsley is involved, that is something we did not sanction. And I give you my word, Captain, that the governor and I have absolutely no knowledge of it.

The three men stood there for a long moment of silence.

"I apologize, Mr. Governor. My remarks and my conduct are inexcusable. I admired and respected Ethan Tyler. He was a great policeman, a great keeper of the watch for the citizens of Connecticut. I'm sorry that I let my emotions get in the way of my sense of duty and honor for your position sir. I would not blame you in the least for not excusing my behavior. You have every right to be insulted by my words. You are my superior and I should have respected that. That, sir, is also what I am paid to do. I didn't do my job.

The governor sat down and bade Sam and Buckley do the same. Cooler heads were going to prevail.

"Sam," began the governor, "I can understand your frustration. I know what it is like to lose someone like Chief Taft. The fact that his murder is somehow involved in all of this has to be very distressful for you.

Twenty-five years ago, I was a senior at Yale and inducted into the Skull and Bones. I thought it was a great honor then and I still do. I know that our motto is 'Skulls above all else', but you must understand that the underlying reason for this motto, the sole purpose for our organization, is to preserve and protect this great country of ours at all costs. This is the very reason such a society as the Skulls exist, no other.

Nicholas Arrington is a great man, and I have his assurance that Mayor Tinsley had no part in this. Nicholas is an old friend. He is an honorable man and I take him at his word. Tinsley is not a member of our organization. It he is guilty, he stands alone. We will not lift a finger in his defense. You have my word on this."

"I'm sorry to have taken up your valuable time, sir. Your word is as good as gold as far as I am concerned. I'm going to leave you two gentlemen and go back and do my job. Thank you both for Ethan. That is very honorable of you."

All three men rose and Sam made his exit. He had exactly the information he was looking for.

"What do you think?" the governor asked Buckley.

"I think that Captain Tyler is one hell of a policeman, sir. I'm sure that his real intention was to get answers and something tells me he got just what he came for."

"I gave Arrington holy hell for identifying with that mouse Tinsley. How on earth did that man ever become a mayor?" the governor wanted to know. "And to bring the spotlight to our organization, well let me tell you, Arrington is skating on thin ice here. More than a few members are concerned about all this. I believe his days as an advisor are ending. If I find out that he is involved in this I'll see that he becomes just an unpleasant memory."

"I fully agree sir. Let's just hope and pray for the best," said Buckley.

"Pray, yes pray. That is a good idea. That bastard Arrington better pray for divine intervention. By the way, I really like that captain. The man has guts. Why couldn't we get people like him to join us? Lord knows, he certainly has the breeding."

Sam went to the reserved parking lot and got into his vehicle. He immediately noticed that the red message light on his two way was blinking, signaling a message. He called the barracks in Westbrook. They informed him that Sergeant Varnish of Old Saybrook Police was looking for him. Sam called the sergeant at the police station in Saybrook.

"You were looking for me, Sergeant?" asked Sam.

"How soon can you get here, sir?" asked the sergeant.

"Inside an hour," said Sam, turning on his lights and siren. "What's up?" he asked as he already had accelerated to eighty-five miles per hour.

"I was cleaning out the chief's vehicle and found two secret compartments full of documents and newspaper clippings. I don't know if it will help, but there sure is a lot of stuff here about this family in Lyme, the Ryans."

"I'm on my way," said Sam as his speedometer hit one hundred miles per hour.

Sam was convinced that Mayor Tinsley was not a suspect. Arrington, however, was another matter. His insistence on Tinsley's innocence only made Sam suspect him even more. Sam had a nagging feeling that Arrington was caught up in all of this, or maybe it was that he just didn't like the guy.

It was a mere thirty-five minutes until Sam's vehicle pulled into the Old Saybrook Police Department parking lot.

"Let's see what you've found, Sergeant," said Sam as he burst through the door.

"It's in the back office, sir," the sergeant informed him.

Sam pulled up a chair at the chief's desk and started pouring through the two folders on it. There were clippings from at least three different newspapers concerning the drowning deaths of two couples during a storm over seven years ago. Their boat apparently hit rocks off Saybrook Point and went down so quickly that no one survived. The two couples were Thomas and Aida Ryan and Ira and Pearl Zuckerman. "Zuckerman" thought Sam. Could that really be a coincidence?

Just then, the sergeant came into the office.

"The chief always had an interest in that case," he told Sam. "I think he just found the whole thing pretty fishy. Facts didn't add up, but he never could find anything to substantiate his suspicions."

"Until now, maybe," said Sam. "Where did you say you found these?" Sam asked.

"I found the first inside the spare tire well," said the sergeant. "The other was in a compartment built into the inside of the trunk door. I'll bet the chief made them both. He was real good with tools. Both contained metal file boxes, to preserve what was inside. Everything was wrapped in cloth to protect them."

As Sam opened the second file, he observed pages of handwritten notes. Ethan had somehow stumbled onto the fact that the real identity of the Ryans was Thomas and Aida Rhineman. A separate article inferred that a third person who should have been on their boat was the Ryan's houseguest Joseph Menger. According to the harbormaster who was there when the party left the yacht basin, Menger was not present. The Ryans had no known survivors, but the Zuckermans were survived by their son, one Nathan Zuckerman of Toronto, Canada. Things were starting to add up. Sam could see that Ethan had never closed the door to the apparent accidental drowning off Saybrook Point almost eight years ago. Just before the murder of Professor Weiss, he must have discovered the real identities of the Ryans. Ethan was one hell of a cop.

If the Ryans were Germans, they must have had a purpose for being in this country. Ethan's notes indicated that there was nothing to substantiate the source of the Ryans' wealth. His inquiries into the State of Washington where the Ryans allegedly came from revealed that there was no proof to the Ryan's claim that they had made their money in land dealings. No one in Washington had ever heard of them. Sam and Ethan came to the same conclusion. German money for German interests. But why? Information, of course. Hitler's people were brilliant. It wasn't too far fetched to construct a theory that an intelligence network had been set up here. Essex was right smack in the middle of a tremendous amount of military activity. There was something else for Sam to consider; another location that made espionage seem more plausible. Bridgeport, Connecticut was a mere eighteen miles south of New Haven and Yale. Bridgeport was a warfare machine manufacturing Mecca. From rifles to airplane engines and everything in between, all were manufactured in Connecticut's most populated city. No one had mentioned it, but there it was, sitting right on Long Island Sound. Sam was convinced that the person or persons involved in the murders were the ones sending radio signals out to Montauk, Long Island.

Sam notified the Coast Guard to be on the alert over the next few days for any small boats heading out to sea. The chances were good that if he apprehended the guilty party here, the whole network would shut down. Whoever was out on Montauk would probably try to get away as fast as possible. Spy crimes were not looked upon too kindly. Getting caught would probably mean certain death. No one, no matter how committed to the cause, would stick around for that.

Sam decided to go back to the Yacht Club to search Menger's boat. He didn't find much. It appeared as though the boat had just been swept clean, much too clean for Sam's liking. The boat was sterile, a sure sign to Sam that something was not right. This was a boat, not a hospital.

It was now time to have a little talk with Nate Zuckerman. Sam drove over to Essex and pulled into a parking space in front of Nate's establishment. There was a "Sorry, gone fishing" sign on the door. Sam tried the door but found it locked. He went around back and climbed the stairs to Nate's apartment, which was just above the shop. That too was locked up tight. Sam went downstairs and tried Meechan's. It was past five o'clock. It was also closed but Sam had a pretty good idea where Bill Meechan could be found.

Sam walked across the street to the Black Swan, where the early evening crowd was beginning to gather. Sure enough, Meechan was seated at his usual spot at the bar holding court with a few of the locals.

"Sam, my boy," said Meechan when he caught sight of him. It was obvious that the hardware store proprietor was getting an early start to his favorite after-work activity.

Sam asked him if he had seen Nate. Meechan had. He observed Zuckerman heading down to his outboard in Middle Cove. He didn't notice any fishing equipment, but that could have already been placed in the boat earlier. Meechan said he couldn't remember the last time Nate went fishing in the afternoon. Before Sam could leave, Meechan put his hand in his pocket and pulled out a shell that Sam recognized as one that was on the floor of Meechan's office at the hardware store. "Damn crazy thing," he said as he gave it to Sam. "Never seen anything like it. Don't know how something like that ever got there."

Sam looked at Meechan and smiled. "I do, William. I do."

Sam went back to the Westbrook barracks to put in a call to Professor Weiss's department head at Harvard. It took three different numbers to track down the head professor who was at home eating dinner; he was happy to be of assistance.

Sam learned that Professor Weiss had traveled to Germany on three separate occasions. The last trip was in 1939, four years ago. The professor also informed Sam that there had been a conference on German relations at Harvard in 1941, before Pearl Harbor and our entrance into the war. The professor told Sam there had been a few incidents that turned into real heated discussions, evenly dividing the pros and cons.

Sam thought for a moment. He asked the professor if there was a record of the attendees. There was. Would the professor be able to get his hands on a copy of it? The professor could do better than that. He could put Sam in contact with the professor who ran the conference. It might take a few hours to reach him, but he promised Sam that he would not disappoint him.

A short discussion with the man led Sam to believe that Professor Weiss was not one of his favorite people. Of course, he didn't want to see him dead, but the thought of Professor Weiss not being part of his department for the fall semester or any semester for that matter was quite delicious indeed. Sam felt sure that the professor would come through. He gave him his home phone number, hung the receiver up and headed for home.

Sam got to Aunt Clara's and called Martha at Ellen's apartment.

"You work pretty fast, cousin," was Sam's greeting from Ellen, who immediately recognized Sam's voice. "You take my best friend, my favorite client, straight out from under my nose. You're good, Sam Tyler, real good."

"Are we through?" Sam asked his cousin. "Can I please talk to Martha?"

"Oh, sure you can speak to your fiancée," said Ellen. "Listen, Sam, all kidding aside, you got yourself one terrific lady. I wish you all the best, honey."

Sam thanked her, and then waited for Martha to take the phone.

Sam asked her how things went and how she was doing. Martha informed Sam that she was going to bring one hell of a dowry to the marriage. They both laughed at that. At Martha's insistence, Sam told her all that had happened concerning the case that day, including the conversation with the Harvard professor and the call he was expecting from another. Neither could wait for Martha's return home. Injun Jim would be waiting for her train to arrive in Old Saybrook at three p.m.

Sam grabbed the steak sandwich Aunt Clara had prepared for him and took the children home. Now all he could do was to wait for a call from Harvard.

The telephone ringing brought Sam out of a deep sleep. He lifted his head off the kitchen table where he had been working on the chart he and Martha had begun a few days ago. Many of the spaces now filled in with the information Sam had gathered up that day.

Sam rubbed his eyes and looked at the clock as he made his way to the telephone. It was twelve thirty a.m. The voice on the other end was from a graduate school associate professor of European studies and economics at Harvard. He apologized for such a late call but explained that he got the call from the department head around eleven o'clock; he had been at a concert, and at the professor's insistence, went to his office on campus to retrieve the information of the 1941 conference. Sam thanked him for his cooperation and made a mental note to call and thank the head professor for his efforts.

Sam learned that Joseph Menger was indeed an attendee at the conference. The associate professor remembered him well. It seems that Menger was a staunch supporter of the Nazi party and that his arguments were so forceful that he almost came to blows with more than one participant. The man shouted Nazi slogans in perfect German and was so disruptive that they asked him to leave. The associate professor vividly recalled Menger yelling in German at the top of his lungs while being carried out forcefully by the police.

"To a tee," was the associate professor's replay. He would never forget Joseph Menger.

Sam listened as the man described the person Sam knew as Nate Zuckerman. It all made sense. Sam thanked him and went back to the kitchen to complete his chart. It all came together. Almost eight years ago, Joseph Menger was a houseguest of Thomas and Aida Rhineman who were friends with Ira and Pearl Zuckerman. It was probably the Rhinemans who were there to set up an intelligence network. They probably befriended the Zuckerman's knowing they had a son who would inherit their business. There is a good chance that Joseph Menger and Nate Zuckerman resembled each other. Sam would call the New Haven police on that one. A short time later, the body of a supposed German male turned up in the railroad yards in New Haven. Immediately after, Joseph Menger, posing as Zuckerman's son, Nate, showed up to assume the family business. Fortunately, for Menger, there was no press present at the Harvard conference. His actions there could have ruined the whole plan. A few years later, a Harvard professor of physics comes to Essex. He's murdered before he can reach Yale to work on some secret project, The Manhattan Project, whatever that is. Sam was convinced that the Manhattan Project was a big deal, or why call a Harvard man to Yale?

This is where things got sticky. The only possible explanation for the series of events that led to Professor Weiss's murder and the following two homicides was that Weiss recognized Menger at the Black Swan and Menger had to kill him. The framing of Robert Rucker was damn smart. Menger might have pulled it off if not for the intervention of Carlton Weimer, thanks to Arlen Templeton, the political aspirations of Jefferson Fine and the whole polluted political climate of the time. Too much self-interest was involved for this to stay a simple homicide and robbery committed by the local town drunk and ne`er-do-well.

And then there was Ethan Taft. Taft's dogged investigations led to his recognizing that Menger had taken on Zuckerman's identity. Menger must have suspected as much because he had to be ready for Taft. There was no other explanation for his ability to kill Ethan. As for the death of the harbormaster, Sam reasoned that Ethan found that odd sailboat, too. And when he realized that it belonged to Menger, he probably asked the harbormaster to call him if Menger showed up. With Ethan dead, the matter should have been moot, but folks in these parts took a dim view of things like murder. The man must have confronted Menger and paid dearly for it. The murder weapon in three of the four homicides was probably the same and it obviously belonged to Menger.

Once again, Sam concluded that Tinsley wasn't smart enough to orchestrate a spy network. Menger could not have been working alone and in all probability was not the brain of the outfit. His tirades up at Harvard proved that. There was someone here pulling the strings. Sam's instincts were that that person was Nicholas Arrington, or at least, Sam was hoping it was. It would make things easier for Sam if it were Arrington. Sam had to admit that he had formed an instant dislike for the man. It's funny how things like that happen for no apparently good reason. Sam could not suppress his desire to wonder what it would be like to land a solid right cross to the large aristocratic jaw of Nicholas Arrington. It was a delightful thought, but one that Sam concluded would really be too good to be true. But Sam was a patient man. Decking Arrington would be well worth the wait.

Sam looked down at the chart and began to appreciate its value. Thank God for Martha and, speaking about Martha, Sam really wished that she were here to share this moment with him. It was her idea that helped crystallize the whole investigation. He wanted her here to thank her for that. Actually he wanted her here for more that that. But that was another story.

Sam dragged himself upstairs to check on the children. He went to his room, laboriously undressed, and collapsed onto his bed. Before ten seconds time had expired, Sam entered the land of nod.

The alarm went off at six-thirty a.m. Even on such limited rest, Sam was up and raring to go. Something told him that this was going to be the day he had been waiting for. He was going to end this whole affair and Ethan's killer was going to experience his last day of freedom on American soil.

Sam ran downstairs and called over to Aunt Clara's house. He wanted to know two things. Was the coffee ready and was Injun Jim around? The answer to both questions was "yes." Sam needed Injun Jim to come over to his place to look after the house until the children got up. He met Injun Jim at the halfway point on the great lawn. Sam asked him to go over to Lyme after the children went to Aunt Clara's and carefully check out the area of the boathouse. If there were any signs of life, he was to get back in his boat and notify Sam.

Sam then put in a call to New Haven but it was too early to reach Matt Donofrio. Sam left him a message to pull the file on the train yard corpse and get back to Sam with a full description as soon as possible. Next, he called Sergeant Varnish at Old Salem Police and left a message for him to call Sam immediately.

Sam could feel his pulse racing. Two quick cups of Aunt Clara's morning java made him feel as though he could use the lawn for a runway and fly down to the Westbrook barracks. "If only Martha were here," he thought. Boy, this was going to be one hell of a day. Sam had no way of knowing how right he was.

Sam got to Westbrook and put in a call to Howard Grimes. They went over every piece of information to double check all their findings. Everything checked out.

"You sound a hell of a lot better than you did the last time I talked to you," offered Grimes.

Sam thanked him for the kind words and for his excellent work on the cases. Grimes was top-notch and Sam really appreciated his work. Sam had gone over the whole kitchen chart to double check everything. Now Grimes had just about sealed the deal.

Sergeant Varnish was the first to return Sam's call. Sam told him to have two boats ready and at least three officers beside himself ready to roll to Hamburg Cove as soon as he got a call from Sam. He also told Varnish to call the Coast Guard on the state police's behalf and have them send people to the same location on the double.

Sam was convinced that he had grossly misjudged the sergeant by his premature assessment of him. Sergeant Varnish's conduct over the past week was absolutely by the book, very efficient police work. He did Ethan proud. Sam was glad Varnish was on board.

Sam no sooner hung up from Varnish than his desk sergeant popped his head through the door to tell him that Matt Donofrio had called from New Haven to say that he had people on it and would get back to Sam shortly.

Sam sat back in his chair. "This was police work at its best," he thought. "Police work the way it's supposed to be." Sam was feeling good. Then he performed two sobering tasks, ones that he had not done in a long time. He went to the gun rack and pulled a pump action single barrel shot from its rack. He checked it for cleanliness and then began placing its large shells in the chamber. Next, he pulled his own service weapon, a long barrel .38 caliber Smith and Wesson and inspected it. Sam took some boxes of bullets and placed them on the desk. Now he had to wait for Matt Donofrio's call and word from Injun Jim.

CHAPTER 12

Martha was all nervous energy at her breakfast meeting with Ellen and her publishing rep at the famous Waldorf Astoria. Louis Laverne, the head honcho at Harcourt Press, lived at the Waldorf. Laverne's family dated back to French royalty and he took over Harcourt some five years ago at the request of the board of directors. Laverne was a kindly but no nonsense elderly gentleman whose family was one of the great French vintners. His management skills were legendary. He didn't need the money, but of course he took the pay and every other amenity that went with the position, although it was really for the challenge that Louis Laverne existed. Long since widowed, with grown sons who looked after the family business abroad, the elder Laverne poured all his energies into the publishing business and yachting, of course.

Breakfast was a joyous affair. If Martha hadn't been in such a rush to return to Essex, she might have more fully enjoyed the efforts of Laverne who actually had the section of the restaurant where they were dining roped off. No fewer than three servers were at his beck and call. Martha did take notice and forced herself to sit and enjoy. Two chefs prepared the food for the five people in attendance. Martha again received another toast with champagne for her wonderful books that were helping Harcourt Press enjoy an exalted position in the publishing world during such trying times. Of course, Ellen's and Martha's attorneys were ecstatic. They were going to enjoy a piece of the action for a long time. It was quite enjoyable to hitch your wagon to a star and make no mistake about it; at this time in this place, Martha Frost was a star. Her star shone as brightly as that of all the movie stars in Hollywood who were living out one and a half hours of entertainment to a hungry public whose country was engaged in a monstrous war. Such names as Cary Grant, Jimmy Stewart, Claudette Colbert, Hedy Lamar and Jeanne Arthur, to name a few, were rumored in the society pages to be vying for roles in the soon to be upcoming movies based on Martha's books; a huge deal had been made for the screen rights. It was further rumored, although no one would substantiate it, that none other than Susan Hayward and Lana Turner nearly got into a catfight at the Copacabana over who would play Martha Frost's heroine. Still, all Martha could think about was getting home to Sam and the children, especially Lillith to whom Martha had grown attached.

Laverne didn't miss a trick. He even notified the press who sent photographers to snatch society news photos that would appear in the Times, the Daily News, the Herald Tribune and many others. This was big stuff. The author Martha Frost had just made a lot of money at a time when most people were happy to have a job at all in the wake of the recent American depression.

Ellen knew what Martha was experiencing, and appreciated Martha thanking her for all the joy that had come into her life. A great new man, whom she planned to spend the rest of her life with, three wonderful children, and now a secure future at what she loved most to do; it was all overwhelming. Martha hugged Ellen, all the while thanking her for orchestrating the whole thing.

"I'll never forget what you've done for me," she told her friend. "I could never pay you for all this."

"Oh, I believe you will," was Ellen's raspy, knowing reply.

Both women laughed and hugged each other tightly.

"Now scoot, the future Mrs. Tyler, or you'll miss your train," said Ellen.

"I'd run all the way back if I had to," said Martha as she turned to run off. "I love you, Ellen Gold," she yelled in full flight.

"I believe she would run all the way," remarked Ellen. "God, I wish I had someone to feel that way about," she thought to herself. "But hell, I'm not about to leave New York. Manhattan is the man in my life."

Martha settled into her seat in first class, compliments of Harcourt Press, and tried to will the engine to start. She was too excited to eat or drink anything. Finally, the train slowly began to wind its way among the myriad of tracks underneath Grand Central until it finally emerged to make its only stop in Manhattan at 125th Street Station. Finally the train started up again, and within minutes, made its way across the East River and over to the Bronx.

"Can't this darn thing go any faster?" Martha's brain was inquiring. It seemed to her that it was hardly moving at all. She closed her eyes and tried to relax. Two forty-seven p.m. was not going to come one minute faster by getting all upset, she reasoned. She'd get there soon enough, then Samuel Tyler was going to have the best wife in the whole world, and those children were going to be spoiled rotten to make up for the years they had lost with their mother. Martha was absolutely committed to her family. And wasn't it going to be great fun to spend time around Aunt Clara, the neatest lady Martha had ever met. How she wished her own mother had not missed the things Aunt Clara had discovered. Family is the most important thing in the world. As far as Martha was concerned intellectualism was a cold, self-serving, loveless existence, except when showered upon oneself. Thank God, the Tylers had saved her from that life. If she had to attend one more writers' gathering at the applicable salons, she was sure she would vomit. Oh well, better just close her eyes and try to enjoy the ride. The pot at the end of this rainbow was made of purest gold.

Sam finally got the call he was waiting for from New Haven. It was Matt Donofrio.

"The damndest thing happened, Sam," said Donofrio. "Someone broke into records and tried to steal some of the files. Almost got away with it too, but the fool took the wrong files. Lucky for us he took so much time. By the time he found the right ones, we nabbed him."

"Another German?" asked Sam half-joking.

"How'd you know?" Donofrio wanted to know.

"Just a lucky guess," Sam responded. "So what have you got?"

Donofrio read the vital statistics of the railroad corpse. Its description sounded amazingly like the man Sam knew as Nate Zuckerman. Sam signed off after thanking Donofrio for his efforts.

As far as Sam was concerned, it was case closed. All he had to do now was to find and apprehend Menger Zuckerman. Sam was beginning to wonder about Indian Jim. He didn't have long to wait, Injun Jim was on the short wave.

"Been here for about four hours and I ain't seen nobody yet. No signs of life either," said Injun Jim.

"Okay," said Sam. "Come back to Wolf Harbor and wait for me. Be careful."

"Don't worry Sam; I left my boat up river. I'm on my way," said Injun Jim. "Got to pick up Miss Frost soon," he reminded Sam.

"Never mind that," said Sam. "I'll see that she gets picked up. You just get back to Wolf Harbor and sit tight."

Sam called the Saybrook Taxi Company to make sure Martha wasn't stranded. He dispatched two Saybrook police officers to the Yacht Club, just in case. All he could do now was to sit tight and hope that Menger hadn't already fled.

After a while Sam drove back to see if there were any signs of life at Zuckerman's. Nothing had changed. He drove down to Aunt Clara's and checked in with Injun Jim.

"You all gassed up?" he asked.

"Topped off," was Injun Jim's reply. "They may outrun me, but they sure can't outdistance me. Trust me, Sam, we're ready."

Sam went back to Aunt Clara's then drove the children up to the Black Swan to visit with Wanda. Sam headed back to the Old Saybrook Police Department to wait things out with Sergeant Varnish who was quickly becoming a favorite of Sam's.

The two forty-seven chugged into Old Saybrook five minutes late. Martha literally jumped off and scoured the platform for a sighting of Injun Jim. She was about to make a few not so complimentary remarks concerning Injun Jim's tardiness when she thought she heard her name being called.

"Martha Frost, Martha Frost," the cries came. "Taxi cab for Miss Martha Frost." "Taxi cab for Miss Martha Frost."

"I'm Martha Frost," she told the man. "Why are you calling my name?"

"Captain Tyler of the state police sent me to take you home, ma'am," said the man. "Here, let me take your bags. Captain Tyler instructed me to tell you to go to Aunt Clara's and wait for him to call you."

"Lead on," said Martha and followed the man to a waiting taxi.

Wanda and the children were enjoying lunch at the Black Swan. Lillith had to go to the bathroom so Wanda took her. As Thomas looked out the window, he caught sight of Nate Zuckerman inside his store with the lights still out. Thomas got up and went outside. Mary followed close behind.

"Thomas, where do you think you're going?" demanded Mary.

"I swear I saw Mr. Zuckerman," said Thomas.

"Oh there you go again. I swear, Thomas Tyler, you're always seeing things. You know better than to leave without telling anybody."

Just then, Nate Zuckerman appeared in the window. He was waving to the children to come over.

"See, I told you he was there," scolded Thomas who looked both ways then crossed the street. Mary was right behind him.

"Were going to get into trouble for this," she announced.

Just then, Martha's taxi started heading down Main Street. Martha saw the children in front of Zuckerman's.

"Pull over here," she ordered the driver. The driver reluctantly obliged. "I'm supposed to take you to Clara Tyler's," he protested.

"Never mind," said Martha who exited the taxi and went to the children.

"What's going on?" Martha asked.

"We were coming to see Mr. Zuckerman. He waved for us to come over," said Thomas.

"We were with Wanda and Thomas left the restaurant without permission," said Mary.

Martha tried the door. It was locked. She looked inside, but saw no one. When she attempted to open the door, the mail wedged into the door fell to the ground. Martha reached down and picked it up. On top was a letter from Nicholas Arrington. His seal on the return address was unmistakable. Before anyone could react, Nate Zuckerman appeared behind her.

"Hi, lads," he said. He quickly moved towards Martha and lifted his shirt slightly so that she could see that he had a weapon in his pants.

"I'll take that mail if you don't mind," he said.

"I'm sure Mr. Arrington would not be too pleased to have this letter fall into the wrong hands," said Martha.

"Smart lady," was Zuckerman's response. "Probably be a good idea to send the children home, Miss Frost."

Martha was only too happy to oblige. "Kids, get into the taxi."

Thomas started to object.

"Thomas, do as I say," she said in a calm but stern voice. "Take the children home," she ordered the taxi driver. "Aunt Clara will pay you."

The taxi driver obliged and started down Main Street to Wolf Harbor.

"You were going to take those children, weren't you?" she demanded.

"Lucky for them you came along, Miss Frost, lucky for me too. I wasn't too keen on taking those kids but until you showed up, they were my only choice."

Wanda Loomis came out of the restaurant just in time to see Nate Zuckerman pull Martha around back. The bartender called Wanda to the phone. It was Aunt Clara.

"What in tarnation is going on, Wanda? Is Lillith with you?" she asked.

"Yeah, Clara," said Wanda, but I don't know where Mary and Thomas are."

"They're with me. They came here in a taxi. They said Martha sent them here and she stayed with Nate Zuckerman. You know anything about that?" she wanted to know.

"I sure do, Clara, but something real strange is going on here. I just saw Nate drag Martha around the back of his place. You better get Sam. I'll get some of the men here and we'll go investigate."

Clara called Westbrook and was informed that Sam wasn't there. "He's over in Old Saybrook," the officer told her. Clara hung up the phone and was about ready to call Old Saybrook, but the phone started ringing. It was Wanda to inform her that some of the men saw Nate's boat with Martha on board going full speed out of Middle Cove.

"Good Lord," exclaimed Aunt Clara. "Get off the phone girl, I've got to get Sam."

Sam picked up the phone to take Aunt Clara's call at the Old Saybrook police station.

"She's what?" yelled Sam. "How on earth did that happen? Never mind, I'll be right there. Tell Injun Jim to be ready to take off." Sam told Sergeant Varnish to get to the boats and wait for his call. He made it back to Essex in record time.

Sam ordered Varnish to take the two boats he had commanded to the mouth of the Connecticut River and not let any boat go out on the Sound without searching it. He told him to be on the lookout for an outboard, driven by a thin man with light colored hair with a woman on board. Varnish alerted the Coast Guard. They had a boat underway.

Sam pulled up to Wolf Harbor where Injun Jim was waiting. Aunt Clara was there with the children.

"He's got Martha," said Lillith through her tears. "Please get her, Daddy," she pleaded.

"Don't worry, we'll bring Martha back safe and sound," he promised. Sam knew Menger was a killer, and that if he went back to Hamburg Cove, there would be no escape. There was no way he was going to lose Martha now. He had to be very careful in dealing with Menger. There was no telling what he might do.

CHAPTER 13

Injun Jim steered the boat out of Wolf Harbor and headed for the high ground north of Hamburg Cove. Injun Jim would wedge his boat in the opening while Sam came in from the north. By now, Varnish and his two boats would be slowly moving up river as per Sam's instructions. The Coast Guard vessel would not be far behind. The trap was set. There was no way out. Now the trick was to get Martha safely out of Menger's hands. Sam's stomach was turning sour. He had to keep control. He couldn't let his feelings get the best of him. He knew exactly what he needed to do and he had to gather himself to do it in a cool, professional manner. As always, a little luck couldn't hurt.

Menger had Martha tied to a chair while he extracted a very expensive Blaupunct radio transmitter from under a hidden trap door.

"Killing adults is not the same as killing children," she said to a feverishly working Menger. "How could you do something like that?"

"Just a minute, here, Miss Frost," said Menger. "Not that I owe you any damned explanations but I would never have hurt those children. I'm sure you can appreciate how desperate my situation is right now, and they were all I had to work with. That is, until you came along."

"Yeah, lucky me," said Martha.

"No, quite the contrary, my dear Miss Frost, lucky me. You saved me from yet another crime that I surely would have regretted. I never meant to kill that fool professor. I just panicked when he threatened to expose me. The man was drunk and he still recognized me. He was talking so loud that I just grabbed the first heavy object I could and hit him with it. That sure shut him up. He had the most surprised look on his face and then he just crumbled. Big bag of wind, he went down in a heap. I thought I killed him."

"What do you mean, you thought you killed him?" asked Martha.

I thought he was dead, so I made a phone call to my superior in New Haven and told him what I had done. He drove up with some men to help dispose of the body. And you know what, the professor wasn't dead. He was lying there and all of a sudden, he started groaning."

"Well, what did you do?" Martha demanded.

"Nothing, that's what I did, nothing at all," was Nate's response. "The next thing I know, the two helpers gather up the professor and take him away in their car. One of them bashes the professor's skull in with a tire iron. But I never saw it happen. I swear, I never killed the man."

"What about Ethan Taft?" Martha continued. "Why did you have to kill him?"

"That was another accident. Ethan saw my superior enter my apartment that night. He must have been staking out my place. My superior had put a gun in my hands. He wanted me to shoot the harbormaster down at the Yacht Club at Saybrook Point. Just my luck, Ethan saw the gun and made a grab for it. He grabbed my arm and it just went off. We both fell backwards and when I crashed into the wall, the gun went off a second time. I know it won't make a difference now; I'm in so much trouble, but I never meant to kill the police chief. I was shocked no one heard the shots. Ethan had put his car around back so no one could see it. One of the men drove the car off while I took Ethan's body over to Lyme and threw it overboard. I really didn't have much of a choice. Things just seemed to go from bad to worse. I'm not a killer, I'll have you know. I just gather information and pass it along. But the harbormaster had been watching my boat with instructions to call Ethan if I ever showed up. Someone down there must have informed my superior about it, so that's why he wanted the harbormaster dealt with. I told him I wouldn't do it. I swear, for a moment, I thought the man was going to shoot me. He sure is real scary and trust me, he won't let anything stand in the way of his plans."

"I believe you already have a pretty good idea who it is. You seemed quite interested in the letter he sent me. I saw the way you recognized the name. That's the reason I came back. Arrington insisted I retrieve that letter before the police did. If it weren't for the damn letter, I would have been long gone. I want you to know something, Miss Frost. It's true I was a loyal German, I really believed in the Nazi party. But then I realized they were going to take on the whole world. That's not what most Germans want. We were just so desperate before Hitler. We believed his lies, but many began to realize, a little too late I might add, that he was a lunatic. But I had no choice. Nicholas Arrington informed me that my parents and my only sister were in the hands of the OSS and I had better cooperate or they would suffer. I have no idea if they are even alive, but I had to do what they told me, hoping to spare my family. However, all that is irrelevant now. I know I'm going to die for what I've done."

Before he said anything else, Sam's voice boomed out through a police bullhorn.

"We know you're in there, Joseph Menger," he shouted. "This is the Sate Police, come out with your hands up. There is no escape. You are surrounded and the river is sealed off. Give it up Menger," he shouted, "it's all over. Let's not have any more fatalities."

Menger went over to the window and fired two rounds from his pistol.

"You're one smart policeman, Tyler. I have Miss Frost in here, Captain. I'll make a trade, but don't try to rush me or I'll shoot the woman."

Sam looked for Injun Jim who made his way up from the river.

"The police and the Coast Guard are about a mile away, Sam," said Injun Jim. The river is all secured. What do you want to do?"

"Can you make your way over to the far side of the boathouse?" asked Sam.

"Honest Injun," answered Injun Jim.

"Good, go over there and see if you can see Martha. I'll make my way to the front. If there's enough room between Martha and Menger, I'll signal you. You create a disturbance and I'll surprise Menger when he turns to go after you," said Sam.

"Sounds good," said Injun Jim who hugged the ground and made his way over to the far side of the boathouse.

Menger was getting very agitated.

He went to Martha and untied her.

"Get up and stand over there," he ordered.

Martha did as he said.

"Why don't you help yourself out and surrender? There's no need to die."

"I'm already dead, woman, can't you see that? Now please be quiet. I've got to think," said Menger.

"The only thing you should be thinking about is how to get out of this thing alive. If what you've told me is true, I'm sure the government will listen to you. I know Sam will," said Martha.

"You know nothing. They're going to kill me for shooting the chief and nothing is going to change that."

"You're wrong," said Martha. "We don't do things like that in America. Why not take your chances and give up?"

"I swear, woman, you're going to drive me crazy. Please be quiet or I'll tie you back up and gag you."

"You're making a big mistake here," Martha continued.

"That's it," shouted Menger.

He slammed his gun down on the table, grabbed some rope, and went to tie Martha up. Instead, Martha grabbed his shirt and using his force rolled her hips over and flipped Menger with a perfect judo throw. A look of shock and pure horror came over the German's face as he found himself flying head over heels. He crashed upside down into the wall and landed on the floor with a mighty thud. He was in too much pain to move. Martha made her way over to the table to take charge of his gun when Sam came bursting through the door. What he saw shocked him.

Menger was lying on the floor, moaning in great pain.

Just then, Injun Jim and Sergeant Varnish came through the back door. They too were taken aback. Everyone looked at Martha.

"What happened here?" asked Sam.

"I neglected to tell you that my research with the New York Police Department included studying judo. I really got good at it," she announced. "Just ask Mr. whatever his name is here."

"See if you can get him up," Sam ordered Sergeant Varnish.

It was a painful effort, but Menger was able to get to his feet.

"Get him back to Saybrook and book him," said Sam. "I'll be right behind you. Have the Coast Guard take charge of the contents of the boathouse and anything in the area they think is important."

Sergeant Varnish followed Sam's orders. Sam went over and took Martha in his arms.

"Doesn't look like you needed my help," he joked.

Just then, Martha's body started to shake.

"Delayed reaction," Martha informed Sam. "I'm great in a crisis, but afterwards, I'm a mess."

"Well, don't be too hard on yourself," soothed Sam. "I'm just happy you had the presence of mind to take care of yourself. Come on, let's get out of here."

Martha placed her arm around Sam and walked out to the boat with him.

The boat ride back to Saybrook Point took about thirty minutes. Sam held Martha all the way.

Sam had Attorney General Buckley notified, but was surprised when Buckley showed up in Old Saybrook as Menger was telling his story. Buckley listened very intently as Menger gave his statement to the recording officer. There was yet another surprise visitor. Carlton Weimer made an appearance. Sam should have known, but he was too busy with his job to take time to consider that both Weimer and Buckley had very good reasons for being there. Weimer should have been there to look after Robert Rucker's interests. That was not the case. The interests of the Skulls brought them both here.

Weimer asked to see Menger's statement before Menger signed it. Buckley agreed, but only after he had read it first. Weimer was agreeable. Buckley finally got his hands on the finished copy, read it and then handed it to Weimer. Weimer sat down and slowly and deliberately read every word. It was obvious that Menger's story aroused his anger.

Sam watched both men with fascination. By now, he had figured out exactly why they were here and what their real concerns were.

Weimer handed the copy to Buckley and nodded his head slightly. Buckley took it and then he and Weimer shook hands firmly. They looked each other in the eye as if to say they agreed. Then they released hands. As Weimer headed for the door, Sam intercepted him.

"You know that if you warn Mr. Arrington, you'll be an accomplice, sir," said Sam.

"Who?" was all Weimer said in response.

"Nicholas Arrington," said Sam.

"Never met the man," said Weimer, who turned and walked out the door.

Sam felt a hand on his shoulder. "I've notified the New Haven Police that you are on your way to apprehend Nicholas Arrington. They'll be standing by to give you every assistance. And Sam, Arrington acted completely on his own. None of us knew what he was doing. We'd never be a party to this insanity. You have to believe me, most of us would gladly die for our country. I give you my word, not one of us will lift a finger to help him. He has perpetrated treason against our country. Now, let him bear the consequences alone. Captain, do your duty. The State of Connecticut stands ready to help in any way we can. Just get the bastard, Sam," said Buckley.

"It will be my pleasure," Sam informed the attorney general.

Sam knew there were only two places Arrington would be. He had a New Haven residence at the Taft Hotel. If he weren't there it was a good bet he would be holed up at the Skull's house on High Street. Sam had called ahead to Sergeant Donofrio to have his people watch both places, but not to act until he arrived. If Arrington attempted to leave, he ordered them to stop him in whatever manner they deemed necessary.

Donofrio understood and dispersed his people. He chose to go to the High Street address. It just made good sense.

Sam put out an all points bulletin for Nicholas Arrington. He notified the police in Manhattan and Long Island where Arrington also resided to be on the lookout. Arrington, considered armed and dangerous, was to be approached with extreme caution. Sam was determined that not one more American would end up dead by the bloodstained hands of Nicholas Arrington.

Sam joined Donofrio at the Skull's house. In a few hours, it would be dark, making the stakeout all the more difficult. One very noticeable characteristic of the home of the Skulls was there were no lights on or near the building. He even noticed there were no streetlights for a hundred feet on either side of the building. Sam smiled, recognizing the irony. All the streets of New Haven were uniformly lit. The break in the pattern told Sam that, clearly, the Skulls had a friend in city hall. It was about ten o'clock when Sam started to get a nagging feeling in his gut. There had to be more than one exit from the home.

"Where can I find a telephone?" he asked Donofrio.

"Forget to tell someone you'd be home late?" Donofrio quipped.

"I need to call that bastard Buckley," said Sam. "I think the attorney general forgot to tell me something."

"Come with me," said Donofrio.

Sam and the sergeant got into Donofrio's police car and drove back towards the campus.

"Forget the school, stop at the first house that has lights on," said Sam.

"You got it," Donofrio responded.

The sergeant slammed on his brakes in front of a large two family house with the first floor light on. Both men jumped out of the vehicle and ran up the steps. Donofrio rang the bell.

"Who is it?" a man's voice came from behind the door.

"Open up, it's the police," said Donofrio.

Very slowly, the door opened and a bald, middle-aged man put his face in the opening with great caution. Donofrio stuck his badge in the man's face.

"We need to use your telephone, sir, it's very important," Donofrio informed the man.

As the man opened the door and stepped back, Donofrio entered and identified Sam.

"Where's the telephone?" asked Sam.

"In the parlor," said the man who was wearing a well-worn bathrobe and slippers that were long past their prime.

Sam grabbed the phone and dialed for information. He got Buckley's number from the operator and dialed it. Buckley's wife answered the phone and was in no hurry to put her husband on the line. Sam informed her that it would not go very well for her husband if he refused to talk to him. Reluctantly, the attorney general took the call.

"I'm going to ask this once and only once. Is there another way to get out of the Skull's house?" asked Sam.

There was no answer.

"Tomorrow, I'm going to get a search warrant to go into that place. If I find another exit, I'm going to arrest you, sir. It's your decision," said Sam.

"Save your threats, Captain. I'll tell you what you want to know, but you must promise that you will not tell anyone about its existence," said Buckley.

Sam took a moment then responded. "You have my word, sir."

Buckley told him about a secret passage that connected the Skull's headquarters to an old abandoned property on the next street. He also informed Sam that Arrington was probably long gone. The loud click Buckley heard was Sam hanging up. He informed Donofrio and they raced to the old building Buckley had revealed.

When they reached the building, they cautiously made their way to the front door. It was slightly ajar. Donofrio began to pull his weapon.

"Forget that," ordered Sam. "Arrington is probably gone. Take me to the train station. Call for some cars to meet us."

Sam and Donofrio raced through New Haven to the train station just as the ten forty-eight was heading south to New York.

"All Arrington wants to do is get out of town. He can get off anywhere down the line and call for help. God knows how many people he could call. We've got to stop him now," said Sam.

"Hold on," said Donofrio. With that, he accelerated and grabbed his two-way radio.

"Call the tower in West Haven," he ordered the officer on the other end. "Do it now," he yelled as he raced down the road that went along the train tracks.

"If the tower can be reached they'll stop the train. I know where it will stop. It won't be going that fast," said Donofrio. The sergeant called for all the cars in the area, even the West Haven police, to meet at the signal crossing station in West Haven. It was now or never. If Arrington got to the next stop, Milford, he could get off and be long gone. There was no telling whom he knew or who would be at his disposal. If they missed their chance, they might never get another.

Sam reasoned that Arrington would have needed time to gather all incriminating documents and any evidence that would reveal the spy network. He had to be on this train. All his eggs were in this basket.

Donofrio had ordered the West Haven police to seal off the east side of the tracks while he and his men would be in front of the train and take up positions on the west side.

As Donofrio pulled his car onto the tracks directly in the train's path he was informed that the tower had responded. The caution lights had been flashed so the train was traveling at a slow speed. Now the light of the engine was visible and the train was slowing to a stop. Police vehicles covered both sides of the train. There was no escaping. The only thing that remained was for Arrington and his henchmen to be on it.

A man jumped from one of the cars and engaged the West Haven police with gunfire. Their return fire left the man lying on the tracks, the victim of many gunshot wounds. He was dead. He was also a decoy. Someone yelled, "fire." Flames burst from the third car back. Arrington had set his luggage on fire. Knowing that escaping with his documents intact was now impossible, he chose to destroy them. He took all the clothing he could from the passengers, as well as the entire carryon luggage and lit them all on fire. It was a smart plan. Arrington knew that a fire would cause panic and that the passengers would flee if allowed. Arrington was happy to oblige. He and his accomplices took off their clothes and exited the train with the fleeing passengers. Arrington's misfortune was in getting off on the west side. Sam and Donofrio had started down that side when the train pulled to a stop. Sam refused to go to the other side when the gunfire by the first man with the West Haven police broke out.

The two fugitives followed some passengers as they approached one of the police cars. Arrington's accomplice wounded a police officer, allowing them to break through the line. Sam and Donofrio were sprinting towards the spot. Donofrio dropped to one knee, aimed and hit Arrington's man. Arrington made it to the other side of the street and disappeared in the marshes that bordered the train tracks. The wounded man retrieved his gun and tried to return fire. A hail of police bullets felled him. Donofrio ran to the road and looked for signs of Arrington. He had escaped into the marshes. Donofrio told one of his officers to finish up and search the train for evidence.

"Come on," he said to Sam as he jumped into one of the nearby police cars. Sam responded and got in as Donofrio was slamming the transmission into gear. He accelerated and burst down the lonely unlit road.

"What the hell are you doing?" Sam demanded.

"There's a small marina just the other side of here. Arrington could swim across and force someone to take him out," Donofrio explained.

The sergeant drove with the lights out and refrained from using his siren. He crossed over a bridge that led to the other side of the inlet and slowed into a tiny boatyard almost obscured from the highway.

"Our man is here, Sam. There's nowhere else for him to go. A boat can spring him," Donofrio declared. "Follow me, there's only one way out to the Sound. Sooner or later he has to go that way."

Sam followed the sergeant, and the two men made their way to a small dock at the end of the boatyard. From here, it was a straight run out to Long Island Sound. There was no time to notify the Coast Guard. Sam and the sergeant took up positions on each side of the inlet. This was their last chance. They didn't have to wait long. A cabin cruiser fitted with fishing gear was slowly making its way towards them. As it got close, the engines erupted and the boat lunged forward. The officers ordered it to stop, but that wasn't going to happen. The boat veered to the left, closer to Donofrio who dove onto the bow as it got near. Sam looked on with amazement as the sergeant made his way to the rear and forced the driver to stop.

Sam was so captivated by the sergeant's actions that he didn't notice a twenty five-foot Cris Craft silently approaching with its lights turned off. Sam crouched to one knee to get a better look and to avoid being seen by the driver who was convinced that his ruse had worked. The man was dressed only in his underwear.

"Give it up, Arrington, this is the police," shouted Sam.

Arrington was startled. For a few brief seconds he appeared to be confused. He reached for his weapon and turned to fire at Sam. Sam fired and struck him twice in the chest and once in the temple. Arrington fell into the wheel and the boat turned and crashed harmlessly into the dock.

By this time, Donofrio and the first boat were approaching.

"You alright?" he yelled out to Sam. "See if there's a woman on board."

Sam jumped onto Arrington's boat. He took Arrington's weapon and made sure there was no other. Next, he inspected the body. There was no pulse.

"Yeah, I'm fine," he yelled back. "Come aboard." Sam went below to find a terrified woman bound and gagged. He assured her she was safe, and then led her up to reunite with her husband. Arrington had told the guy that if he didn't do as he said, he would kill the woman. The guy was near hysterical, the sergeant explained.

In less than twenty minutes, the dock was alive with police presence. The press was not far behind. Donofrio made sure that someone brought him and Sam fresh coffee.

"You did real good work there, Captain," Donofrio said.

"Yeah, thanks to you," said Sam. "What the hell were you thinking, jumping onto a moving boat like that? Aren't you a little old to be doing stuff like that?"

"Hell, I'm in my prime," Donofrio responded. "Just wait till this war's over and we play you farmers again. We'll see who's a little long in the tooth, my friend."

Both men shared a laugh, and then Sam got serious.

"I really wanted that guy, Matt. If it weren't for you, he would have gotten away. I don't know if I could have lived with that," said Sam.

"I think we make a pretty good team if you ask me, Mr. State Police Captain. It was a pleasure working with you," said Donofrio. "Sam, I know you and Chief Taft were close. I'm glad I could be the one who helped you out here. Just remember this, my friend; you have a good friend right here in New Haven. You're always welcome here, Sam. You're a good man and a real good cop. It was an honor working with you. I'm sure Taft would be proud of you. You did good, my friend, you did good."

The two men shook hands and hugged. It had been one scary night. But now it was over and Sam couldn't wait to get back to Wolf Harbor to Martha and the family. He got a ride to his car and drove back to Westbrook to file his report.

CHAPTER 14

It was three a.m. when he pulled into his driveway. He walked the path to the patio and started to head for the door when he noticed Martha asleep on one of the lounges. He walked over, sat down on the edge and tenderly stroked her hair. Martha peered through sleepy eyes to see that it was Sam.

Sam took her in his arms.

"Did you catch the bad guy?" she asked.

"Yes," said Sam. "Unfortunately I had to shoot him. Too bad, because he should have stood trial as a spy and a traitor."

Sam held Martha and looked up at the star filled sky. "It's all over," he said. "Ethan can rest and we can get on with the rest of our lives."

Martha woke as the sun came warmly into her room. She realized that she had slept fully clothed. She vaguely remembered Sam walking her to Aunt Clara's, but had no idea how she had managed to climb the stairs to her room. Obviously, she made it to her bed, but she really could not remember anything else.

Martha washed up, changed, and went downstairs to join the family for breakfast. Sam was already there, working on his first cup of Aunt Clara's morning brew. The children were all dressed and ready for breakfast.

"What day is it?" Martha asked.

"It's Saturday," answered Sam.

"Wow, I've lost all sense of time and proportion," said Martha. She took her seat between Lillith and Sam as Aunt Clara placed a large plate of scrambled eggs on the table.

"Oh brother, look at me," said Martha as she got up to help Aunt Clara serve the breakfast. The breakfast table was a beehive of conversation.

"I have an idea," said Sam. "The Italian festival is on Wooster Street tonight. How about we all go into New Haven?"

Everyone agreed it was a great idea, except Aunt Clara; she never did stray too far from Essex. And the thought of being in the company of hundreds of strangers was too much for her to cope with. No, she'd stay here and just enjoy the peacefulness of her home, for once. She looked forward to it.

Sam went to the barracks to check in and follow up on his report. He called Howard Grimes in Meriden as a matter of police procedure.

"Glad you got these guys, Sam. I know how much this meant to you," said Grimes. "Word's out that Buckley's really tooting your horn. Don't be surprised by anything that guy cooks up. Take care, pal."

"Buckley," thought Sam. Got to give him a call. It took two separate calls. Buckley was up at the state capitol. He was happy to take Sam's call.

"Great work, Captain," he shouted into the phone. The governor is ecstatic. Sam, you really saved the day."

"I had help sir," said Sam.

"Hell man, you're too modest. You're the talk of Hartford. What can I do for you, Captain, why the call?" Finnelly asked.

"I wanted to apologize for last night. Things were a little chaotic and I guess I got a little carried away," said Sam.

"Nonsense, Sam. You did your job. The State of Connecticut owes you a debt of gratitude. Hell, the whole country owes you one. You shut down a major spy organization and got all the guilty parties, to boot. I'd say you ought to be pretty damn proud of yourself. I wouldn't be surprised if the President, himself, got in on this. This is big stuff, and you're the reason it happened. Enjoy your day in the sun, Captain, believe me, those days are far and few between. Take care, Captain, we'll be seeing you soon," bellowed Finnelly who then hung up.

Sam sat there in amazement. No matter which side of the coin people like Buckley was on, they always seemed to come out right side up.

Sam and the family reached Wooster Street in the Italian section of New Haven around six p.m. The sun was still shining and people enjoying the festivities filled the street, to say nothing of all the fabulous Italian food offered by the many food vendors. Four blocks of Wooster Street were aglow, illuminated by hundreds of gaily-colored strings of lights strung along the street poles and on every building along the way.

Lizzy and Peter Childers met them and Martha introduced them to the children. Peter was especially charming. He got along wonderfully with the children, particularly Thomas. They began to eat their way up one side of Wooster and down the other. As soon as it got dark a band playing Italian songs on a makeshift stage prompted many of the old timers to begin dancing. Everyone was having a great time.

Then Sam caught sight of Matt Donofrio making his way over to where he and the family were standing.

"I heard you'd be here," said Donofrio.

"Hey, Matt, what brings you here?" asked Sam.

"You," said the sergeant directly.

Sam introduced Sergeant Donofrio to everyone.

"We need to talk," he said. "Can you get away for a little while? I wouldn't ask if I didn't think you'd be interested."

Sam checked with Martha who assured him that she and the Childers would look after the children. She told him to go, she'd be fine.

Sergeant Donofrio walked Sam over to his police car and drove across town, not saying much of anything. Then Sam recognized that they were on High Street. They drove past the Skull's house and then around to the back. As they pulled up to the building in the back that was used as a secret entrance for the Skulls, he was met by a great surprise. Sam could not believe his eyes. The building had burned to the ground.

Sam and the sergeant got out and walked through the rubble to the place where the doorway was.

"Watch your step, Sam," Donofrio cautioned as he led the way into the passageway. The passageway went in about ten feet and then ended abruptly. It was blocked by a stonewall.

"How long has that been here?"

"My guess is no more than twelve hours. The stones look new to me. They must have had some masons put it up before they burned the building down."

"You think the Skulls did this?" asked Sam.

"Well, I didn't do it. Did you?" asked the sergeant.

Sam shook his head and walked out to the street.

"These people are capable of anything, aren't they?" said Sam.

"They're just a fact of life for us lowly public servants here in New Haven, Sam. I just thought you should see this. You're the one who went up against these people. You won, this time. You're lucky, most people don't win when they come against them. You have their respect, Sam, that's something. But walk softly with these people. They're not used to losing and they're not very good losers."

Sam remembered Arlen Templeton telling him to tread softly also. Sam knew how fortunate he had been. This time, luck, or the fates, were on his side. He would do well not to tempt the fates in the future.

"Where did you go?" asked Martha.

"The sergeant wanted to show me something," said Sam.

"Was it important?" she asked.

"Important enough to tell me how lucky I am and how precious you all are to me," Sam told her.

Just then, Peter, Lizzy and the children came away from the ice cream stand to join them.

"Come on, gang, let's go listen to the music," said Sam.

As they walked through the growing crowd to the far end of the festival, many thoughts were racing through Sam's mind. It had turned out to be a great summer. The weather really had cooperated. Martha had come into his life to fill a deep void left by Sally's death. Once again, the pure joy of sharing love with someone had miraculously come his way. He would probably be promoted and definitely decorated. For a few weeks anyway, he knew that he would be the darling of the press. Who knows, he might even get to see the President. Buckley was not one to speak idly. The whole idea could be quite intoxicating. Still, there was one sobering reality. The Skulls were now very aware of who Samuel Tyler was and what he was capable of. No one knew exactly how many members the Skulls had or even who those members were, but they were not the kind of enemy anyone would want. In a world of uncertainty, you could be sure of one thing; the Skulls would always be watching.

THE END